MURDER AT ROCHESTER PARK

A 1920S COZY MYSTERY

CATHERINE COLES

ABOUT THE AUTHOR

The daughter of a military father, Catherine was born in Germany and lived most of the first 14 years of her life abroad. She spent her school years devouring everything her school library had to offer!

Her favourites were romance and mysteries. Her love for the Nancy Drew books led Catherine to check out every mystery story she could find. She soon found Agatha Christie who quickly became Catherine's favourite author.

Catherine writes cosy mysteries that take place in the English countryside. Her extremely popular Tommy & Evelyn Christie mysteries are set in 1920s North Yorkshire while her new Martha Miller mysteries are set in the 1940s in Berkshire.

Catherine lives in northeast England with her two spoiled dogs who have no idea they are not human!

You can find Catherine online at www.catherinecoles.com

If you would like to be amongst the first to know about her new releases, price drops, competitions, and special offers, please join Catherine's newsletter - details can be found on her website.

Books by Catherine Coles

The Tommy & Evelyn Christie Mysteries

Murder at the Manor
Murder at the Village Fete

Murder in the Churchyard
Murder in Belgrave Square
Murder at the Wedding Chapel
Murder in India
Murder at the Seaside (a novella)
Murder at Docere House

The Martha Miller Mysteries

Poison at the Village Show

This is a work of fiction. Names, characters, places and incidents either are the product of the author's imagination or are used fictitiously. Any resemblance to actual persons, living or dead, events, or locales is entirely coincidental.

Copyright © 2022 by Catherine Coles

All rights reserved. No part of this book may be reproduced or used in any manner without written permission of the copyright owner except for the use of quotations in a book review.

First paperback edition March 2022

Edited by Sarah Miller & Annetta Jackson
Book design by Sally Clements

ISBN 978-1-915126-05-4 (ebook)
ISBN 978-1-915126-06-1 (paperback)
ISBN 978-1-915126-14-6 (large print)

Published by Inspired Press Limited
www.catherinecoles.com

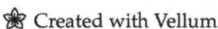 Created with Vellum

CAST OF CHARACTERS

Main Characters

Tommy Christie - The 7th Earl of Northmoor, former police officer

Evelyn Christie - Policewoman during the Great War, Tommy's wife

The Family

Lady Emily Christie - Tommy's great-aunt
Hugh Norton-Cavendish - The 9th Earl of Clifford
Elise Norton-Cavendish – Hugh's wife & Lady Victoria's eldest daughter
David Ryder – Tommy's Solicitor
Madeleine Ryder – David's wife & Lady Victoria's younger daughter
Constance Christie - Tommy's sister
Grace Christie - Tommy's sister
Henry (Harry) Christie - Tommy's brother

The Guests

Alexander Ryder – The 10th Earl of Chesden (David's elder brother)
Albert Lewis – Local business owner
Louisa Lewis – Albert's wife
Stanley Cameron – Albert's assistant
Peter Balfour – Albert's solicitor
Clara Balfour – Peter's wife
Edwin Granville – Albert's accountant

Emma Mountjoy – Albert's secretary

The Staff

Wilfred Malton - The butler
Phyllis Chapman - The housekeeper
Mary O'Connell - The cook
Jack Partridge – Tommy's estate manager
Doris - Evelyn's maid
Elsie Warren - Nanny/nursemaid
Joe Noble – Hessleham Hall's gardener

Others

Detective Inspector Gregory – Senior detective from Derby
Detective Sergeant Bishop - Junior detective

CHAPTER 1

Christmas Day, 1922 - Derbyshire

"It's like being at home." Aunt Em accepted a drink from the butler, Malton, then turned back to Evelyn. "Except not as comfortable."

"Ssh," Evelyn admonished, though privately she agreed.

The drawing room at Rochester Park, the home of the 9th Earl of Clifford, was much like the rest of the house – faded, dilapidated, and draughty.

"If I should freeze to death tonight, please make sure I am buried in my peacock blue dress. You may, of course, have my mother's ruby and onyx necklace."

Evelyn quickly smothered a grin. "It's not that bad."

"Perhaps it isn't for a young thing like you with a husband to keep you warm. But for an old lady like me, hypothermia is an actual concern."

"Aunt Em!"

The old lady waved a hand. "Please don't act so outraged, Evelyn. I am not being uncouth, but simply stating a fact. Two people together will stay warmer than one by themself."

"Good evening, everyone!" Elise called out from the doorway. "I do hope you are all comfortable."

"Lady Clifford." Malton gave a slight bow as Elise Norton-Cavendish, Tommy's cousin, and the new bride of the 9th Earl of Clifford, walked into the drawing room. "May I make you a drink?"

"Please be kind, Aunt Em. Elise is trying so very hard," Evelyn whispered as she noticed the high colour in Elise's cheeks and the overly enthusiastic smile that stretched the younger woman's lips.

"Thank you, Malton. I should very much like a glass of tonic water with ice."

"Tonic water with ice? I suppose that's easy enough for Malton to supply. He can chip it off the insides of the windows." Aunt Em raised her eyebrows pointedly at Evelyn as though something had just occurred to her. "Surely the child isn't—"

Evelyn gripped her glass a little too tightly and tried not to think about the assumption Aunt Em had quickly arrived at. There could be many reasons Elise wasn't taking a drink before dinner, but Evelyn easily recalled how her sister, Millie, couldn't stomach alcohol with each one of her pregnancies.

Elise smiled at Evelyn and Aunt Em before walking over to Albert Lewis, a local business owner who had finagled an invitation to the Boxing Day shoot at Rochester Park that was to take place the following day. Before lunch, Elise admitted to Evelyn that she didn't much like Albert and hoped that her new husband, Hugh, wouldn't do business with him.

However, as expected of a dutiful hostess, she was speaking to him before anyone else in the room.

"I can't think where Hugh has got to," Aunt Em said in a quiet voice. "It's too bad of him to leave poor Elise to a room of guests by herself."

"He's with Tommy," Evelyn replied. "Discussing the arrangements for the shoot in the morning. Hugh is incredibly nervous."

"You've brought your entire staff, horses, and your dogs." Aunt Em raised an eyebrow. "I don't know what the boy thinks can go wrong when he has all the help you and Tommy have provided for him."

"You have just commented on the house." Evelyn took a sip of her drink. "Having expert help will go a long way to making this event a success."

"I do hope Madeleine has brought plenty of blankets for the baby." Aunt Em adjusted the rug covering her lap. "This house is so much colder than Hessleham Hall."

Evelyn patted Aunt Em's hand. "You don't need to worry about Josephine. She has so many knitted hats and cardigans she'd be warm if she was in the Arctic."

"Humph." Aunt Em glanced out of the enormous arched windows. "If I didn't know better, I'd think we were in the Arctic."

Outside, snow fell in pretty flurries, which Evelyn thought was a blessing in disguise. It hid the neglected gardens that hadn't enjoyed the care of a gardener since before Hugh's father died.

Financial constraints had prevented Hugh from keeping on more than a skeletal staff and were the primary reason behind him entertaining a man such as Albert Lewis. It was an open secret that Hugh's father, the 8th Earl of Clifford, had been a notorious gambler. Although the coroner recorded his death earlier that year as an accident, no one who knew him believed his death to be anything but a suicide.

Perhaps he thought his death would help Hugh, but it had only left him with more problems as he struggled to support his mother in her London home and make his country estate in Derbyshire financially viable.

Tommy and Hugh entered the drawing room. While Malton fixed their drinks, Hugh made his way over to his wife. Evelyn noticed the adoring look Elise gave him as she caught hold of one of his hands. He was very lucky to have found a wife who would stand shoulder to shoulder with him through his troubles.

"How are my two of my most favourite girls?" Tommy asked as he stood next to the Queen Anne sofa on which Evelyn and Aunt Em were sitting.

"Is everything alright?"

"Of course, darling," he answered lightly. "Why wouldn't it be?"

"Elise isn't keen on Albert Lewis."

Tommy twisted his lips in consternation. "Hugh says he's a rather boorish man but he may be forced to do a deal where he sells off part of his estate to the man to cover death duties."

"What will Mr Lewis do with the land?"

"That's the problem," Tommy said. "Lewis intends to build a housing development on it."

"A housing development?" Aunt Em wrinkled her nose in distaste as she looked at Albert Lewis. "What type of houses?"

"Terraced homes, apparently." Tommy accepted the glass of brandy Malton offered him. "As many as he can fit into the available space."

"Oh no, that wouldn't do at all." Aunt Em shook her head. "Goodness only knows what characters could end up living at the end of the lane. Poor Elise."

"I don't think Hugh has much choice."

"Can he not sell the land with conditions stipulating what Mr Lewis can and cannot do with it?"

"He's tried that," Tommy said. "That was the first thing David suggested to him. However, Lewis is adamant he wants to use the land for houses."

David Ryder was an old schoolfriend of Hugh's and married to Elise's sister, Madeleine. He was also an accomplished solicitor who left his lucrative practice in London to marry Madeleine and settle in the north of England, where he worked primarily for Tommy though he did have a few other clients.

Tommy looked around the room. "Have you seen Constance?"

"Not since lunchtime." Evelyn exchanged a nervous look with Aunt Em. "I'm sure she's just taking her time getting ready for dinner. You know how young girls are when they want to look their best."

"I'd be a lot happier with that explanation if I could see Alexander Ryder!"

"Now, darling," Evelyn said placatingly. "I'm sure there's nothing to worry about."

"Don't you remember what was going on under our noses when we stayed at our London house earlier this year?" Tommy's face flushed. "I shall kill him if he takes advantage of my sister."

"I remember the last time you uttered those words," Aunt Em said in a conversational tone. "The person to whom you directed your threat was murdered."

Tommy's hand, resting on Evelyn's shoulder, tensed at his great aunt's words. "I wasn't the perpetrator on that occasion, but if he dares overstep—"

"Look," Evelyn said. "Here they both are."

Constance's face was flushed, the tip of her nose red. Her smile faltered as she met her brother's glare.

"She's been outside with him, the little fool." Tommy's voice was harsh. "If any harm should come to her—"

Evelyn reached up and squeezed his hand. "I'm sure they simply wanted a moment alone without everyone's attention on them. You do remember what it was like to be young and in love, don't you?"

"Yes," Tommy replied grimly. "That's what worries me."

They were called to dinner, which prevented Tommy from saying any more, but she was certain he would seek Alexander out after their meal to speak to the young man.

*E*lise rushed to Evelyn's side in the corridor. "I'm desperately sorry, Ev, but I've sat you next to Mr Lewis. I couldn't think of anyone else who would be unfailingly polite to him."

"Who have I got?" Tommy asked his cousin.

"Clara Balfour on one side, Emma Mountjoy on the other."

"Mrs Balfour is the wife of Mr Lewis's solicitor, is that right?"

"That's it," Elise said. "Miss Mountjoy is Lewis's secretary. She's a quiet mouse of a thing. As you can imagine given she works for such a fellow."

"Jolly strange to bring one's secretary to an event like this," Tommy said.

"I believe he's determined to complete the deal he's offered Hugh." Elise put a hand on Tommy's arm. "That's why he needed his solicitor, assistant, accountant, and secretary to be here. You won't let him rush into anything, will you?"

Privately Tommy thought Albert Lewis was taking advantage of Hugh and Elise's hospitality. "Hugh wants to provide for you."

"I know, he's incredibly sweet, but he must be sensible."

"I think he's trying to be realistic, Elise. His father's death has left him in an impossible position."

"You will help us, won't you?" Elise's pretty face looked drawn, worry lines standing out starkly on her forehead.

"That's why I'm here." Tommy hoped the authority in his voice would reassure his cousin. "Evelyn and I will do everything we can to guide and advise you and Hugh."

Elise nodded, but the obvious concern didn't leave her expression. "We're very grateful for everything you're doing for us."

As Elise hurried into the dining room, Tommy hung back to speak to his butler. "Can you do something for me, Malton?"

"Of course, Lord Northmoor."

"Please ensure any drink you serve my brother after dinner is watered down. The last thing we need is a repeat of my mother's wedding. Lady Clifford has enough to worry about."

Malton inclined his head. "Certainly, My Lord."

Harry, Tommy's teenaged brother, had been so intoxicated the evening before their mother's wedding that he had gone missing. The last thing Elise needed to worry about in the morning was the safety of her guests.

He took his place at the table and nodded at the two women on either side of him.

Clara Balfour was a very pretty, petite blonde. Emma Mountjoy, on the other hand, was a plain woman with dark hair and a habit of hunching her shoulders as though she was trying to make herself smaller. It was an impossible task as Emma stood at almost six feet tall.

"Good evening, Mrs Balfour, I hope you are enjoying your stay at Rochester Park?"

"Thank you, Lord Northmoor. I am. It's a beautiful old house."

The old part was certainly accurate. Whilst it may have been a lovely house once, it was anything but now. The weather certainly didn't help. Wind whistled throughout the old manor house, and curtains fluttered, giving it a rather eerie feel.

"Will you be joining us at the shoot in the morning?"

"I don't shoot." Clara Balfour shuddered. "Neither is it the type of activity suitable for a woman in...that is to say, I would not feel safe tramping all over the countryside in snow."

"Enough said." Tommy smiled at the woman, guessing

what she'd been about to say. "Congratulations to you and your husband."

"Thank you." She looked down at her empty plate, a faint flush staining her cheeks. "Peter and I have recently moved up from London. I'm not sure I shall ever feel comfortable participating in traditional country pursuits, if the truth should be known."

"I understand. Outside activities are not for everyone."

"Indeed, My Lord." Clara smiled gratefully, seemingly relieved that they would not expect her to join in. "Do you and your wife have children?"

"No." Tommy's response was quick, but the stab of pain at the question was as sharp as ever. "We have not yet been blessed."

Alexander Ryder, on Clara Balfour's other side, asked her a question then, saving her from finding something else to say to Tommy. He swallowed his hurt and turned to the lady on his right. "How are you finding your time at Rochester Park, Miss Mountjoy?"

"I'm looking forward to tomorrow," she said eagerly. "I understand Lord Clifford's new dogs are a present from your wife?"

"That is correct," Tommy replied, glad to speak on a subject which allowed him to extol his wife's virtues. "I'm proud to say that my wife's gundogs are by far the best in the north of England."

"They are Gordon Setters, is that correct?"

"That is correct," Tommy said. "Despite the name, they are gundogs. Lady Northmoor trains them to fulfil all the necessary functions of hunt, set, and retrieve."

"How fascinating," Emma Mountjoy replied in a voice that suggested she meant what she said. "I should very much like to speak to your wife about her training methods."

"She would enjoy that very much, Miss Mountjoy. Any

opportunity she has to discuss her beloved dogs makes her very happy indeed."

"I know you, don't I?" The strident voice carried across the table and Tommy looked over to see who Albert Lewis was addressing. The businessman waved his soup spoon in the air, seemingly toward Clara Balfour.

She frowned. "I don't believe so, Mr Lewis."

"Yes, I do," he insisted. "I thought so yesterday when we arrived. Now I'm sure. Your hair is different, but we've definitely met before."

"Clara is my wife, Mr Lewis," Peter Balfour spoke up. "Perhaps you've seen her at my office? She often visits me at work, don't you, dear?"

"Perhaps that is it," Mr Lewis said doubtfully, his eyes still pinned on Clara.

The awkward moment passed as Evelyn engaged Albert Lewis in conversation. However, he looked back across the table at every opportunity, a frown on his ruddy face.

Conversation hummed around the table comfortably until the staff served dessert. Tommy wasn't close enough to see what happened, but Albert's chocolate and vanilla blancmange somehow ended up in Elise's lap.

"I say!" Hugh got to his feet. "That's dashed careless of you, Lewis!"

The larger man tried to school his features into a blank look, but he failed. His lips twitched before he broke out into a loud guffaw. Tears pooled in Elise's eyes as she looked down at the mess on her lap.

"Oh, Albert." Louisa Lewis looked horribly embarrassed.

Frank Douglas, the first footman, jumped forward with extra napkins. He held them out to Elise, a look of consternation on his face – the poor fellow clearly did not feel comfortable helping her to mop the mess but felt as though he should do more to help alleviate the situation.

Evelyn hurried to Elise's side. Grabbing the napkins from

Elise, she scooped the mess from Elise's gown and put the soiled linen onto the floor. She then pulled the young girl to her feet.

"Come along, let's go upstairs. I'll help you change."

Tommy watched as his wife hurried Elise from the room. However, she wasn't quite quick enough to hide the tears streaming down Elise's cheeks.

"You owe Lady Clifford an apology when she comes back downstairs," Tommy said stiffly as he pinned Albert Lewis with a glare.

"Yes, yes, of course." He waved a hand in front of his face, knocking over his glass. Red wine spread across the white tablecloth, drawing gasps from other diners.

Tommy glanced at Hugh. The other man's face was thunderous, his good manners clearly the only thing stopping him from exploding.

"Not sure what all the fuss is about," Albert muttered. "I can't be the first man to be a little merry."

It seemed Tommy had asked Malton to water down the wrong man's drinks.

~

Later that evening, Tommy and Evelyn made their way upstairs to bed.

"The evening improved," Evelyn ventured.

"It could hardly get any worse," Tommy retorted. "Poor Elise. Was she desperately upset?"

"I'm afraid she took it all rather personally." Evelyn grimaced. "The poor girl didn't dare take a drink so she could remain completely in control of her first dinner party as a married woman."

Tommy shook his head. "And that drunken buffoon Lewis ruined it for her. If Hugh was against doing business with him before dinner, he'll certainly do everything in his power to avoid it now."

"Hopefully tomorrow will go off without a hitch," Evelyn said as they reached the top of the stairs. "If Hugh can raise the profile of Rochester Park as an excellent venue for shooting, perhaps he can start charging patrons and raise some money that way."

"I think that's an excellent idea," Tommy agreed. "But it will barely make a dent in what he owes, I'm afraid."

"I wish—" Evelyn didn't finish her sentence as a piercing scream filled the air.

"What on earth is going on?"

A door crashed open further up the corridor and Tommy rushed towards the disturbance, with Evelyn close behind him.

Louisa Lewis, Albert's wife, staggered into the hallway, clutching the lapels of her dressing gown across her throat.

"Mrs Lewis?" Tommy questioned. "What can we do to help?"

"It's Albert," she panted. "Oh, it's dreadful! I think he's dead."

Evelyn rushed past Mrs Lewis into the bedroom and stopped as she reached the stocky figure of Albert Lewis, who lay prone on the carpet.

Tommy rested a hand on Evelyn's waist as he peered past her at the body. "There's not really any doubt that he's dead, is there?"

"No one could have skin that colour and survive," Evelyn said. "Oh, Tommy, it's repulsive."

He moved past her and kneeled next to Albert. Placing two fingers on his neck, he looked up at Evelyn and shook his head. "You're right, he's definitely dead."

"Has he had some sort of seizure?"

"Perhaps."

Evelyn moved past Tommy into the bathroom. "There's a

medication bottle on the floor. The lid is off, and there are tablets scattered all over the floor."

"Is it his?"

She examined the label on the bottle. "Yes. Some unpronounceable name. It says take one tablet three times a day."

"You haven't picked it up, have you?" he asked from the doorway.

Evelyn levelled Tommy with a scathing look. "Don't be ridiculous. I simply crouched down and looked at it closely."

"What is it?" Elise's voice asked desperately. "What's happened?"

Tommy moved out of the way as Evelyn hurried back into the bedroom. Despite her haste, she was too late to prevent Elise from seeing the prone figure of Albert Lewis.

"I'm so sorry, Elise."

"Is he dead?" her voice shook as she lifted fear-filled eyes to Evelyn's.

"I'm afraid so," she replied. "Is there a key for the bedroom door?"

"A key?" Elise repeated, then shook her head. "I don't understand."

"I think it's best if we lock the door and secure the evidence until the police get here."

"The police?" Elise looked over at Tommy. "Of course. I must telephone for them at once."

"Where's Hugh?" Tommy asked.

"I don't know." Elise's chin wobbled. "He told me to come up to bed and said he would be right behind me."

"Come along with me." Tommy caught hold of Elise's arm. "I can make the call, if you would prefer?"

"Yes. I think you should." Elise looked at Evelyn. "Are you coming with us?"

"I'll stay with Mrs Lewis," Evelyn answered. "She will need to take some of her belongings from the room. I can see there is a key in the door. I shall lock it and bring Mrs Lewis downstairs with me."

Constance moved forward out of the group of people that had come out of their rooms to see what the commotion was all about. "Can I help, Evelyn?"

"Perhaps you could put the kettle on?" She glanced at Mrs Lewis, who stood shaking next to the door. "I fear it's going to be a long night."

"Of course." Constance hurried off along the corridor behind Tommy and Elise.

Evelyn moved over to Louisa Lewis. "Mrs Lewis, would you like to take some clothes out of your room?"

The woman shrunk away from Evelyn and looked at her as though a particularly nasty smell emanated from every pore. "I cannot go in there. Not while—"

"Let's go downstairs." Evelyn reached out a hand. "My sister-in-law has gone to—"

"Do not touch me!" Mrs Lewis shrieked. "My Albert was fine until he came to this house. You and your friends are to blame for this!"

"Me?" Evelyn asked disbelievingly.

"One of you has killed him!" Mrs Lewis's voice rose with every word. "My husband was poisoned!"

"What is his medication for?"

"Oh, wouldn't you like it if he died because of his high blood pressure?" Mrs Lewis backed away from Evelyn. "You didn't see him. He took his tablets as usual, then started grasping at his throat as though he couldn't breathe. He went a terrible purple colour and dropped to the floor."

It sounded a little like a heart attack to Evelyn, but she wasn't about to argue with the bereaved woman.

She pulled the door closed behind her and twisted the key in the lock. "I think it best we all gather in the drawing room while we wait for the police to arrive."

"Yes, the quicker they get here, the better," Mrs Lewis spat. "Otherwise I'm certain I will be the next one poisoned."

"Poisoned?" Grace, Tommy's youngest sister, whispered. "Has that awful man really been poisoned?"

"I'm sure he's had a heart attack," Evelyn said soothingly.

As she walked towards the stairs, a trickle of unease tickled its way down her spine. Despite her words to Grace, and her immediate belief that Mr Lewis's death was natural, she couldn't help but be affected by the strength of Louisa Lewis's conviction that someone had killed her husband.

CHAPTER 2

"I am Detective Inspector Gregory from the Derbyshire police force, and this is my colleague, Detective Sergeant Bishop. We have, of course, been called out because of a sudden death." The detective beamed incongruously at everyone gathered in the drawing room. "I'm sure there is nothing for anyone to be concerned about, but we shall do our best to look into the circumstances of Mr Lewis's death as quickly and unobtrusively as we can."

The man had an air of competence about him, but it didn't soothe Louisa Lewis. "My husband has been poisoned. I don't know why everyone refuses to listen to me."

"Why do you say that, Madam?" The detective turned his shrewd gaze on the widow.

Tommy watched as a self-satisfied look crossed Louisa's face before it cleared and left one that could only be described as enthusiastic and indulgent. Here was a woman who clearly enjoyed being in the spotlight.

"My husband was perfectly healthy until he took his blood pressure tablets."

"In actual fact, he was rather drunk," Hugh retorted. "Perhaps a man with medical issues should not overindulge his love of alcohol."

"Albert was a little clumsy this evening," Louisa said, fighting to regain the detective's attention – he was now looking at Hugh with interest. "Under the circumstances I think it's jolly poor form you insinuate that his accident at dinner had anything to do with his alcohol consumption."

"Forgive me," Hugh replied in a tone that showed he didn't care which way Mrs Lewis took his words. "But your husband was drunk, embarrassed my wife, and then laughed as though his actions were amusing."

The detective held up a hand. "I'm not sure any of this is relevant. Now, I intend to go upstairs and look at the scene. A uniformed officer will stay here to ensure no one leaves the room."

Why did detectives do that? Partly to assert their authority, he was sure. Tommy hoped he had done nothing so ridiculous. It was pointless making everyone stay in one room when it had taken the police hours to arrive. Anyone who wanted to hide anything had plenty of time to do that before they arrived.

Evelyn got to her feet. "Excuse me, Detective Inspector Gregory?"

The detective stopped at the doorway to the drawing room and turned to look at Evelyn. "Yes, Madam? What can I do for you?"

Tommy flinched at the detective's patronising tone. Evelyn pulled back her shoulders before she spoke. "I have the key you will need to enter Mr Lewis's bedroom."

"Why do you have the key? I believed Mr Norton-Cavendish to be the owner of Rochester Park."

"Lord Clifford is indeed the master of the house," Evelyn said in her usual quiet, efficient, and unfailingly polite way. "I am simply a guest who happened upon the scene shortly after Mr Lewis's collapse. I thought it prudent to lock the door to ensure everything remained untouched until you arrived."

He raised his eyebrows and coolly assessed Evelyn. "Do you have knowledge of police procedures?"

"A little. I worked for my local police force in Yorkshire during the war."

Evelyn's words were delivered with pride, but Tommy saw the detective's expression turn to dismissive indulgence before he spoke again. "I'm sure you were a great help, Madam."

Tommy moved to Evelyn's side, unable to stand the condescension in the detective's voice. "I would ask that you refer to my wife correctly as Lady Northmoor, and not Madam. She has also, very modestly, neglected to tell you about the occasions over the last few years we have assisted the police in their duties."

"I'm too busy to keep the titles straight. I hope that won't be a problem for you."

"Of course not," Tommy replied smoothly. "May I ask, what is your Christian name?"

"Arthur." The detective shook his head. "What does that have to do with anything?"

"My wife will give you the key, Arthur. Perhaps you will think about her quick thinking while you are upstairs and remember to thank her when you return."

"I don't care who you are, you can't call me Arthur!" he spluttered.

Tommy held out his hands, palms up. "I just did, Arthur."

The detective reached out a hand and stabbed Tommy in the chest with his outstretched forefinger. "I will not stand for anyone interfering with my investigation, regardless of what their title is. Anyone who gets in my way, or does not respect my authority, will be arrested. Do I make myself clear?"

"Perfectly, Arthur."

The detective looked around as the sound of amusement

rippled around the large room. He made one last attempt to reassert his control. "I insist you address me as Detective Inspector Gregory."

"Of course, Detective Inspector Gregory," Tommy said easily. "All I ask is for the same courtesy when you speak to Lord Clifford's family and guests."

The detective had the good grace to look suitably chastened. "It's so hard to keep track of who is who."

"Try," Tommy told him firmly. "No one really cares if you get it wrong, but it's rather lazy and discourteous not to make an attempt, especially if you expect the same consideration."

"Point taken," the detective replied through clenched teeth.

As soon as the detectives left the room, Aunt Em clapped her hands together. "I do so enjoy it when you act masterfully, Lord Northmoor."

"I will accept no one being rude to my wife."

"You were very gallant, darling." Evelyn squeezed his hand.

"I am aware you do not need me to come to your rescue," he said. "But there are occasions when I cannot, and will not, stand back."

"Have you people listened to yourselves?" Louisa Lewis asked, disdain dripping from her words. "My husband is lying upstairs dead and all you care about is whether your proper title is used."

"I secured your bedroom," Evelyn replied, "so that if your husband has been killed, as you claim, the police can examine any evidence without the risk that it has been tampered with. For that reason, if no other, I think we should all be respectful to each other."

"Oh, drat," Edwin Granville muttered. "I seem to have lost a cufflink. And goodness only knows what I've done with my eyeglasses."

"Your glasses are on top of your head," Emma said indulgently. "I'm sure your cufflink won't be far. Perhaps Lady Clifford would be so kind as to ask her maids to look out for it."

"You always have the right answers, Miss Mountjoy. What a delight you are." Edwin turned to Elise. "I would be most grateful, Lady Clifford, if your maids could keep their eyes out for my cufflink."

He got to his feet, fiddling with his remaining cufflink as he walked over to Elise. "Here, it will be just like this one."

As he struggled to remove it from his buttonhole, it flew through his fingers and landed in Elise's lap. A collective intake of breath echoed through the cavernous room.

Elise plucked the silver jewellery from her dress. "I must say, Mr Granville, this is the most pleasant thing to land on me this evening. It's caused much less mess than blancmange too."

Tommy smiled at Elise's expert handling of the situation. She had come a long way from the sulky girl he first met at his London home in Belgrave Square earlier that year.

Edwin Granville, the dead man's accountant, was an older gentleman whose somewhat eccentric personality seemed to be directly at odds with Albert Lewis's hard-nosed business ethos.

"You, young woman!" Louisa Lewis said in a strident voice, ensuring all eyes turned back to her. "What do you have to say for yourself?"

"Me?" Clara Balfour asked as the other woman pointed her way and she became the centre of attention.

"Yes. My husband clearly recognised you at dinner and you pretended you didn't know him."

"I assure you I had never seen him before arriving at Rochester Park."

"How can that be?" Louisa choked out a mirthless laugh. "Your husband has worked for Albert for years, has he not?"

"That is true," Clara said coolly. "But I don't make it a habit to accompany my husband to work."

"Then Albert must know you from somewhere else," Louisa persisted. "He never forgets a face."

"Perhaps I simply remind him of someone else," Clara said dismissively.

"I shall be watching you." Louisa pointed at the younger woman. "I do not trust you. No, not one little bit. You are hiding something. I mean to get to the bottom of it, let me tell you."

"Mrs Lewis, would you like to take a seat?" Detective Inspector Gregory came back into the room, his expression grave.

"I would not." Her face set into stubborn lines.

"Very well," he said. "It is my sad duty to confirm that I believe your instincts regarding your husband's death are correct. That is to say, both the doctor and I are as sure as we can be that Mr Lewis was poisoned. There will be a post-mortem to verify this, of course."

"I knew it!" Louisa gloated and looked around the room triumphantly. Belatedly, she seemed to realise a widow should have an appropriate emotional response to the news their husband had been killed. Gloating certainly was not expected. She dramatically sank into a wing-backed chair near the fireplace and pulled a handkerchief from her reticule. "Oh, my poor Albert. He didn't deserve this. No, he certainly did not. Oh, what shall I do without my Albert?"

She dissolved into noisy sobs though, Tommy observed, there was not a single tear to be seen.

~

"Well, what do you make of that?" Tommy asked as soon as he and Evelyn entered their bedroom.

"I think Mrs Lewis is already counting her money." Evelyn took the shawl from around her shoulders and folded it neatly on the chair near the window. The curtains rippled, and she shivered. "Goodness, Tommy, I shall never complain about the heat we lose in Hessleham Hall ever again. Sometimes I feel as though we are standing outside braving the elements."

Tommy snapped his fingers. "That reminds me. I must talk to Ryder in the morning."

"David?"

"You know very well I mean Alexander."

"We took many walks outside alone when we were courting."

"You did not have an elder brother to look out for your welfare," he answered. "I have asked him several times not to do anything that would compromise Constance's reputation."

"Perhaps you're speaking to the wrong person," Evelyn suggested gently.

"Whatever do you mean by that?" Tommy flung his jacket on top of her shawl and paced to the other side of the room.

"Constance is a very persuasive young lady. You may find that she has encouraged Alexander to break the rules you set out so clearly for him."

"They're not rules, they are suggestions."

"And what happens if he ignores your *suggestions*?"

"We have a man-to-man talk and I explain his misunderstandings to him clearly. I gave him permission to court my sister, not to gallivant around outside alone with her."

"Are they to court entirely in the presence of others?"

He looked at her with surprise. "Of course."

"We didn't."

Tommy's lips twisted. "Which is why I am so concerned about Constance."

"I understand, and applaud, how seriously you take your

role as your sister's champion. Not having one, however, didn't do me any harm."

"I was a gentleman."

"You were not always as perfectly behaved as you would want Alexander Ryder to be." Evelyn walked over to her husband and wrapped her arms around his waist. "I'm not saying you shouldn't talk to him. But, perhaps, remember what it is like to be young and in love."

"I'm still young and in love," he murmured against her hair.

"Then you should understand perfectly how a young fellow like Alexander feels."

"Must you always be so reasonable?"

She leaned against his chest and smiled, even though he could not see her face. "Yes. Especially when you're about to make a mistake in judgement."

"Hmm." He rubbed a hand down her spine. "Let's talk about something else. Do you think the widow Lewis may have something to do with her husband's death?"

"I'm not sure about that, but I do feel that she isn't at all upset by his passing. At least, whatever sadness she feels is tempered by how rich she will be."

"I agree. What are your thoughts on Clara Balfour?"

"I think there might be something for us to look at there."

"You do?" Tommy put his hands on Evelyn's shoulders and leaned back so he could look into her face. "I thought she seemed rather embarrassed at Lewis's insistence that he knew her."

"She was certainly embarrassed." Evelyn nodded. "But that doesn't mean his recollection wasn't accurate."

"He was drunk!"

"Again, I agree with you, but I thought he was genuine."

"So we have suspects already," Tommy said. "Mrs Lewis could have killed her husband for his money, and Mrs Balfour to stop him from saying where he knew her from."

"Of course, for that to make sense, she must have a particularly nasty secret she didn't want him to reveal."

"I wonder what made the doctor and the detective so certain Lewis was poisoned." Tommy frowned.

"Perhaps he will tell us in the morning?"

"He doesn't seem the sort that will share any information with us. Particularly if he thinks we will involve ourselves in the investigation."

"Which, of course, we will."

"I don't see how we can't," Tommy said. "This is the last thing poor Hugh needs. He wants to raise the profile of Rochester Park so people will want to come here for shoots. Certainly not because it's the site of a murder."

"I feel desperately sorry for Elise." Evelyn turned around. "Could you undo my zip please, darling?"

"Wait a moment." He went into the bathroom and returned with his robe. After unzipping her dress, he wrapped her in his warm robe. "I thought dinner went very well. Apart from dessert, of course."

"Having the senior members of our staff here definitely helped Elise." Evelyn pulled back the thick blankets on their bed and climbed underneath. "She can see how a household should be run."

"How long do you think you will stay?"

"As long as it takes to find staff and help Hugh train his puppy." She lifted a shoulder. "You don't mind, do you?"

Tommy got into bed beside her and leaned over to kiss her brow. "I think it's very kind of you to offer to help Elise find the right people to help her run the house."

Evelyn gave a small laugh. "Hugh really does not know what to do with the dogs, either. In fact, I think it is he who will need me more than Elise."

They had agreed before travelling to Rochester Park that Evelyn would gift Hugh two of her dogs – one an older dog that she had fully trained and the other a puppy. Hugh was not keen on the idea of charging shooting parties to use Rochester Park, but even he could see that he must make use of every opportunity to raise money if he wanted to keep his land intact.

Tommy smacked a hand against his forehead. "I didn't even consider what Lewis's death will mean for Hugh. The land deal is unlikely to go ahead now."

"He didn't want to sell to Lewis anyway, did he?"

"He didn't," Tommy confirmed. "But now he doesn't have that option. Selling that parcel of land would have allowed him to pay off the debts his father accrued and start some renovations Rochester Park requires. He was reluctant, but also realistic."

"Let us put aside our worries for a while, Tommy," Evelyn suggested. "It won't be long until we have to be up for breakfast, and the detective has insisted they must question us. We must use our own powers of investigation, otherwise Hugh won't have any choice about paying guests in his home – no one will want to come here."

Tommy pulled a face. "Or everyone will want to come, but for the wrong reasons."

She hadn't even considered that people would want to come to see where a man was murdered, but some were ghoulish like that. They might even want to sleep in the room of the murdered man. Evelyn shuddered. That would be positively dreadful.

∼

"Ryder, I would like to speak to you!" Tommy called to Alexander as he tried to sneak out of the dining room after breakfast.

"I rather thought you might."

"As you like walking outside so much, let's take a turn around the house." Tommy walked toward the front door.

"Are you going outside, My Lord?" Malton asked.

"Yes. I would like my coat and Lord Chesden's, please."

Malton gave instructions to the footman, who hurried off to fetch the warm outer garments for the two gentlemen. Tommy didn't need to turn around to reassure himself that Alex had followed him from the dining room. They stood next to the elaborately decorated Christmas tree in the hall whilst they waited.

When they were outside, Alex turned to Tommy immediately. "I expect this is about last night."

"It most certainly is," Tommy said. "Was I not clear about how exemplary I expected your behaviour to be around my sister?"

"Constance wanted—"

"I do not wish to hear what my sister wanted." Tommy turned to him, temper flaring inside him. "You are a gentleman. Any fault is yours, none is my sister's."

"She can be incredibly persistent."

"I am sure. Yet it is your responsibility to ensure that her reputation remains unsullied by anything you, *or she*, may do."

"I understand that," Alex replied. "We didn't walk any further than the spot in which we are standing right now. I swear we did nothing which would cause you concern."

"Yet I am concerned," Tommy retorted. "I know I cannot judge your character solely based on our initial meeting earlier this year. However, your attitude then, particularly towards women, means I feel I must take extra precautions with my sister's happiness."

"I am not the same man now as I was then," he said earnestly.

"If I believed you were, we would not be having this conversation," Tommy returned.

The front door closed heavily and Tommy turned to see

Detective Inspector Gregory coming down the stairs towards them.

"What are you doing out here?" he barked at them angrily.

"I wasn't aware taking a stroll outside was out of bounds," Tommy said easily.

"You're not really strolling," the detective retorted. Tommy didn't reply – the other man clearly had something to say, otherwise he wouldn't have come outside himself, he would've sent one of his underlings. "Which is a good thing. I would hate for you to interfere with our evidence."

"If there's evidence out here, we should have been told." Tommy looked out across the snow-covered lawn and saw, for the time, what he should've seen immediately. A set of footsteps was clearly visible. He tried to recall what time it had stopped snowing the previous evening, but he could not. Had he really been so distracted worrying about Constance that his usually inquisitive mind was not noticing things he would ordinarily take notice of?

"I had a man stationed on the front door." Frustration lined the detective's face. "You should have been prevented from leaving the house."

"If you had deigned to inform either Lord Clifford or myself, we would not only have been aware of your wishes, but ensured my butler was also vigilant." Tommy glanced back at the house. "What happened to your chap?"

"I found him in the kitchen." The detective grimaced. "He wasn't able to resist your cook's shortbread."

Tommy grinned – that he could understand. Mrs O'Connell baked the best goods he had ever tasted. "Would you like me to explain to the guests that they should stay inside?"

The detective opened his mouth to speak, seemed to think better of whatever it was he was going to say, and took a deep breath. "I think perhaps we got off on the wrong foot."

"I apologise for my part in that," Tommy said affably. "I

can never stop myself from defending my wife, though she is more than capable of speaking for herself. As I am sure you will find during the course of your investigations."

"I would like to speak to everyone together," the detective said. "What is the best way to do that?"

"Oh, I should think sounding the gong will bring everyone into the hallway." Tommy walked back towards the house. "They will be confused as it is not time for luncheon, but I am certain they all will come quickly enough."

CHAPTER 3

"What's happening?" Evelyn descended the stairs and moved over to Tommy's side. "Who sounded the gong?"

"The detective," he answered. "He wanted everyone gathered together. There's a set of footprints in the snow across the lawn. Perhaps he wants to find out who they belong to."

"Surely they are Alexander and Constance's?"

"No," he said. "Alexander is insistent he and Constance stayed close to the house. In any event, there's only one set."

"What's the relevance, do you think?"

"Absolutely no idea." Tommy's brow furrowed. "Let's go find out."

They filed into the drawing room. The detective stood in front of the fireplace, a particularly uncompromising look on his face. His detective sergeant stood to the side. It dismayed Evelyn to see a uniformed police officer close the door then stand in front of it. She wasn't accustomed to being on the outside of investigations. Usually, she and Tommy were ahead of the police when it came to finding out clues. On this occasion, it appeared Gregory and his colleagues knew much more than they did.

"There are footprints in the snow across the lawn," the detective said, with absolutely no preamble whatsoever. "I need to know most urgently who they belong to."

"I took a short walk with Miss Constance Christie yesterday evening," Alex Ryder offered. "Neither of us, however, went across the lawn. We stayed on the path close to the house."

"Did you see who did?"

"I thought I'd seen someone," Constance spoke up, then shook her head. "But it was so dark, I'm sure now it was a shadow from the shrubbery."

"Someone *was* out there." The detective's eyes bore into Constance. "Tell me everything that you remember."

Evelyn watched the girl as she struggled to recall exactly what had transpired the previous night. "Lord Chesden and I went outside. I thought I heard something. It was just a vague impression of a sound, nothing concrete or specific you understand."

"Did either of you investigate further?"

"We didn't." Constance slid a glance towards Tommy. "Lord Chesden said something that distracted me, and I thought nothing more of what I heard until now."

"Anyone else?" His small brown eyes scanned the room. Although his intense scrutiny caused a few people to shuffle in their seats, no one responded. Eventually, when it seemed certain no one else was going to speak up, he gave a small nod. "Then I must assume whoever walked across the lawn yesterday is the person who entered the gardener's shed, removed potassium cyanide and used it to doctor Mr Lewis's medication."

Louisa Lewis's head fell forward, so her chin almost rested on her chest. "How unspeakably cruel. What did Albert ever do to anyone?"

Albert Lewis was a thoroughly unlikeable man, but he did

not deserve to die – especially in such an excruciatingly painful way.

"Lord Clifford, I will need to speak to your gardener as a matter of urgency. It appears, at least from the footprints, that the shed was accessed after the snow stopped falling yesterday afternoon."

Hugh sat down heavily on a chair. "We don't have a gardener."

"That is to say, our previous gardener retired," Elise said. "We didn't think it was worth our while engaging someone new until the spring. There's so little a gardener can do during the winter."

It was a brave attempt to save face, but Evelyn doubted anyone believed Elise. Those of a certain class may not discuss their financial difficulties openly, but that didn't mean they were not public knowledge.

"In that case, I will need the name of your previous gardener so I may find out exactly what was inside the shed."

"Of course." Hugh got to his feet, visibly shaken by the news that Albert had been deliberately poisoned by cyanide found on his property. "I shall go into the study to write his information out for you."

"May I ask, Detective Inspector," Tommy said. "How do you know the tablets were altered?"

"We arrived at the conclusion incredibly easily," the detective said smugly. "Both the doctor and I smelled bitter almonds when we examined the body, an irrefutable sign that cyanide had been used to kill him. Although some care had been used to separate the parts of his blood pressure capsules, we could see clearly they had been tampered with. Of course, we await the test results to confirm the cyanide was placed inside the capsules, but that is our working theory."

"Wicked," Mrs Lewis muttered and buried her face into a handkerchief, sobbing loudly. "Poor Albert. What a terrible way for him to go."

Clara Balfour was the first person to verbalise what that meant for the assembled guests. "That means there is a deadly murderer here in this room. How perfectly dreadful."

Her husband put an arm around her shaking shoulders. "I demand that we are given permission to leave this house. My wife is in a delicate condition."

"No one is leaving," the detective said firmly. "Not until I get to the bottom of this deplorable crime."

"We must—"

The detective held up a hand. "Mr Balfour, please. I understand your concern for your wife, but no one will leave this house until I say so. I will begin interviewing everyone immediately and make a further statement when all interviews have been concluded."

Mrs Lewis wasn't the only one who liked to be the centre of attention. It seemed the detective also enjoyed everyone's eyes on him. However, he seemed rather more competent than others in his position.

"I assume we are free to move around the house?" Evelyn asked.

"Yes, indeed." The detective turned his slightly amused gaze onto Evelyn. "You may go wherever you would like inside, but no one must leave the house, for any reason. Do I make myself clear?"

"I'm afraid that will cause me a problem," Evelyn said calmly.

"Why is that, Lady Northmoor?"

"We have dogs in the house that require access outside for sanitary reasons. I'm sure you understand."

Anger flitted across his expression before he breathed deeply through his nose. "How has this been arranged until now?"

"I have a maid, Doris, who exercises and cares for my dogs whilst I am busy. I believe she, and one of Lord Clifford's maids, have been regularly taking the dogs outside since our arrival."

"How have they been getting out of the house?" he thundered as he looked at the uniformed police officer standing next to the door.

Evelyn wasn't certain he wanted her to answer the question, or whether he was addressing his colleague. "They take the dogs out of the side entrance, Detective Inspector."

"Did I not give precise instructions that no one was to leave the house?" he ignored Evelyn as his voice rose in volume. "Why were those instructions so difficult to follow?"

"I...we...that is none of us thought you meant to include the staff."

"You're not paid to think," Detective Inspector Gregory barked. "You have been on the force long enough to know that you should leave that type of high-level work to the detectives."

Hugh returned with a sheet of paper, which he handed over to the detective, oblivious to the heightened tension in the room as the uniformed officer was humiliated in front of everyone. "Our former gardener's details."

"In my day," Aunt Em said into the embarrassed silence. "One had the good manners to give a dressing down, if it was required, in private. I regret to see those days are over."

The detective stared at Aunt Em for a long moment, then turned to Hugh. "Lord Clifford. I should like to speak to you first. We shall hold our interviews in your study."

Hugh didn't look happy about the detective's decision, but in his usual affable way, he agreed gracefully. "Of course."

David Ryder got to his feet. "May I ask, Detective, on what basis are you speaking to Lord Clifford?"

"This is his house. He knows better than anyone else what we can find on the premises. It's no secret he disliked the victim, especially after the unfortunate event during dinner last night."

He was certainly knowledgeable about the events of the previous evening. Evelyn wondered who had told him what had happened. She was certain it wouldn't be any of her staff. They were loyal and discreet.

"Then you are not simply *speaking with him*, but treating him as a suspect?" David phrased his sentence as a question, his voice raising on the last word as he waited for the detective's response.

"He is currently my primary suspect. I see no reason to hide that." The detective extracted a notebook from his pocket and consulted it. "Who are you?"

"Mr David Ryder," he said confidently. "I am the family's solicitor, and I insist I accompany Lord Clifford during any, and all, questioning."

Evelyn looked down at her lap to hide a smile at the detective's look of complete frustration. David Ryder was engaged to work on behalf of Tommy, but because Hugh was married to Tommy's cousin, 'family solicitor' was technically correct.

"Very well." The detective managed the two words through gritted teeth, his lips barely moving.

"Perhaps you will be so good as to furnish a list to your detective sergeant giving the order you would like to speak to the guests? Then they can make themselves available to you at the correct time?"

"Are you people going to interfere at every opportunity?" the detective made one last attempt to regain control. "Or am I able to run my own investigation?"

David held out a hand towards the door. "Let's get this over with, shall we? Lord Clifford is an extremely busy man."

The detective looked as though he wanted to say more. Perhaps he was going to point out that it was Boxing Day, and the only thing Lord Clifford and his guests had on their calendar that day was the traditional shoot.

Evelyn wished it were possible for it to still take place, but she thought better of mentioning it while the detective's patience was already stretched thin. Perhaps it wasn't a good idea to have a shoot while there was a murderer lurking amongst them – she remembered all too well what happened at Hessleham Hall the previous year during a summer event shoot when a villainous murderer was on the loose.

~

As the detective ushered Hugh from the drawing room, Aunt Em got to her feet. "I call a family meeting."

"A family meeting?" Tommy echoed.

"In private," Aunt Em clarified, then pointed at Alexander Ryder. "You are included. Come along, we shall talk in the library."

Tommy exchanged a look with Evelyn. "What is she up to?"

"I think we are about to find out. Knowing Aunt Em, it will be contrary to the orders the detective has given."

They settled in the library – Tommy's sisters Constance and Grace, brother Harry together with Elise, and Alexander Ryder.

"Should I fetch Madeleine?" Elise wondered.

"Is she in the nursery with the baby?"

"Yes, but Elsie is there too. She can take over and look after Josephine if we need Madeleine down here with us." Elise smiled at Evelyn. "I'm not sure why you employ a nursemaid, Ev. Madeleine is a very attentive mother."

"Josephine is a very lucky baby," Evelyn said. "She has a wonderful mother and a very competent nursemaid when required. There are times when Madeleine simply can't be with the baby, so having Elsie is certainly necessary in my opinion."

Evelyn didn't need to add that it was her dearest wish Elsie would one day be busy with more Christie babies – one of whom she and Tommy hoped desperately would belong to them.

"We can talk to Madeleine later," Aunt Em said. "Now I'm sure we all agree that the detective is hopelessly out of his depth in investigating this crime. Tommy, I insist that you and Evelyn solve this murder so Hugh can have his shoot, and we can all get back home safely before New Year."

"He's very clear he doesn't want anyone to interfere," Tommy said, then grinned at his aunt's stern expression. "Though, of course, we have never let that stop us before now and I'm sure I speak for Evelyn when I say that we will not let his directives prevent us from involving ourselves on this occasion."

"I'm very glad to hear that," Aunt Em said. "I am afraid that the detective will try to make the facts fit his theory and arrest poor Hugh for the murder simply because this is his house."

"We can't let that happen." Elise reached out and grabbed Tommy's arm. "Oh, please, Cousin Tommy. You won't let that happen, will you? Hugh wouldn't hurt anyone despite how dreadfully Mr Lewis behaved last night."

"We will do everything we can," Tommy assured her.

"Elise is right. Hugh doesn't have it in him to hurt another human being," Alex said.

Aunt Em assessed Alex Ryder. "You, on the other hand, Lord Chesden, would do anything you needed to in order to keep your family safe. Am I correct?"

He inclined his head. "That is so, Lady Emily."

"Then your role is to protect the ladies of this family while Tommy and Evelyn are busy doing what they do best. Do you accept this role?"

"I am proud and privileged that you trust me to carry out such a duty, Lady Emily," he answered gravely.

"So there we are, Tommy." Aunt Em's pale blue eyes twinkled. "It is time for you and Evelyn to get to work."

"How exciting!" Constance smiled at Tommy. "What can I do to help?"

"Stay inside with your brother and sister and keep safe."

Constance bowed her head demurely, but he didn't miss the amused look on her lips. "Yes, Tommy. I promise I shall do as you ask and stay as close as I can to our protector."

"Indeed." Tommy struggled to keep his voice, even despite his sister's taunting words. For the first time, he had some sympathy with Alexander Ryder – his sister was incredibly headstrong. "Though he is to keep his eyes on all of you, which means there will be no repeat of last night and sneaking outside by yourselves."

Constance looked as though she had more to say. Tommy floundered for words of caution that would not cause his sister to do the very opposite of what he'd asked of her.

To his delight, Evelyn stepped in. "About last night. You said you thought you had heard something but were then distracted?"

"It was probably an animal in one of the bushes," the young woman said dismissively.

"Perhaps," Evelyn agreed. "Though given what we know now, it is possible it was the murderer going over to the gardener's shed to get the poison he or she used to kill Mr Lewis."

"Do you really think that is possible?"

"Yes," Evelyn said seriously. "That is why it's so very important that you stay close to your family. If the murderer has even the slightest impression that you may be able to identify them, you could be in danger."

Fear for his sister made Tommy push the matter further, even though he could see Constance was concerned about her safety. He didn't miss the fact she had taken a step closer to Alexander Ryder. They were now in such proximity their shoulders were practically touching and their hands, dangling by their sides, were less than an inch apart.

"You told the detective at first that you thought you'd seen something, or at least a shadow, that could have been a person. Now you're saying it was only a sound. It's extremely important, Constance, that you try to remember precisely what happened."

"We went outside before dinner." Constance glanced up at Alex and smiled shyly. "I thought I saw something in my peripheral vision. I turned my head in that direction, then Lord Chesden said something to me, and I turned my attention back to him."

"I don't suppose you saw or heard anything?" Tommy asked Alex.

"I confess all of my attentiveness was on your sister."

Tommy took a deep breath before responding. "As entrancing as she is, I must implore you to be more vigilant going forward. I am trusting you implicitly."

Alex adopted a look of complete subservience that Tommy wanted to wholeheartedly believe in, but he couldn't help but still be wary of the other man. "I take the safety of your entire family seriously. You can trust me, Lord Northmoor."

"We trust you much more than the police," Evelyn said. "Do you know that the policeman who was supposedly on guard at the front door was tempted away from his post by Mrs O'Connell's shortbread?"

Everyone laughed, which was certainly Evelyn's intention. Tommy found it difficult to join in. "If anyone wants shortbread, they must pull the bell. No wandering off to the kitchen, please."

"You're becoming rather tiresome," Harry said. "We understand we must be careful. We are no longer children."

Unfortunately for his siblings, that's exactly how Tommy saw them. Now that they lived with him rather than their mother, they were also his responsibility and he took that as seriously as he did all of his duties.

~

*T*he morning passed quickly as the police took the family and guests into Hugh's study to interview. Although Tommy and Evelyn had spoken to Hugh and Elise after their meeting with Detective Inspector Gregory, they had not talked to anyone else.

Evelyn hoped conversation at luncheon would provide an opportunity to find out more about the guests. Although the meal was less formal than dinner the evening before, everyone was still gathered together in the dining room.

Louisa Lewis pushed her plate away. "I can't eat that."

"Oh dear," Edwin Granville said with a worried frown on his elderly face. "Is there something wrong with the food? I say, it hasn't been poisoned, has it?"

Cutlery clattered onto crockery as everyone stared at Edwin in dismay. Elise deliberately carried on eating. She paused, looked up, and chewed her food. "The food is delicious. I shall not be wasting it, though what each of you choose to do is your own affair."

Louisa Lewis, clearly furious that her thunder had been stolen yet again, pushed her chair back from the table. "I shall tell everyone I know what a positively awful time I have had here."

"As I have already said to you privately," Elise said calmly, "I am desperately sorry for what has happened at Rochester Park. It is particularly difficult for you to lose your husband at Christmas time. However, neither I nor Lord Clifford, or indeed our home, can be held responsible for your husband's untimely demise. The culpability for that lays in the hands of the person who brought about his death."

"I concur wholeheartedly," Aunt Em said. "Well said, my

dear. It's ludicrous to suggest that Lord and Lady Clifford bear any accountability for what has happened. Neither should they suffer any ill will as a result."

"My husband's death is only one issue I have faced while staying here," Louisa said sulkily. "My bedroom is draughty, there is mould on the ceiling in my bathroom, and the food is completely unpalatable."

"I find the food first rate," Edwin chimed in, his earlier concern about his meal being poisoned clearly forgotten.

"That is because you are accustomed to eating what your housekeeper feeds you and she's even older and more senile than you," Louisa muttered churlishly.

"What was that, m'dear?" Edwin put a hand around his ear. "You know I don't always catch what you say if you don't enunciate clearly."

Louisa waved a dismissive hand in his direction. "Oh forget it. You will only hear me if I talk about money."

"Eh?" He leaned forward. "Did you say something about Albert's will?"

A self-satisfied smile settled on Louisa's face. "I didn't actually, Edwin, but that is a jolly good idea. Peter, is that something you can arrange?"

The solicitor's face showed his repulsion for Louisa's question. "I don't think now is really the time."

"I am his widow, you are his solicitor. It isn't for you to tell me when the time is correct, it is for me to tell you."

"Well…" he stuttered. "Well…I am uncertain of the correct protocol in a situation like this."

"It's really rather simple," Louisa said scathingly. "You worked for my husband. He is no longer with us, so until I say otherwise, you now work for me. And I say I want the will read. Today."

"I understand that, and I don't believe I am giving anything away by saying you are a named executor," he said, gathering some of his lost composure. "However, I will have to check with Detective Inspector Gregory that he sees no reason it can't take place today as you wish."

Aunt Em, sitting next to Evelyn, tapped her arm and leaned closer. "That's not right."

"What isn't?" Evelyn whispered back.

"One doesn't refer to a woman who administers an estate in that way. She is an executrix. Not an executor."

"Perhaps it's a unisex term?" Evelyn wrinkled her nose in distaste. "One finds those used so often these days."

"You must speak to David immediately," Aunt Em advised. "I do not trust that man."

"Mr Balfour seems very nice."

"People are rarely what they seem, Evelyn. You have seen the evil things some of them do to their fellow humans enough times now."

"I shall make speaking to David a priority," Evelyn reassured Aunt Em.

She scanned the faces of those around the table. Louisa looked incredibly happy with herself, but to Evelyn's surprise she wasn't the only one exhibiting what she thought were unexpected emotions.

Peter looked concerned, Clara frightened, Edwin completely indifferent, whereas Emma's expression could only be described as gleeful.

The will of Albert Lewis had nothing whatsoever to do with Evelyn, but she determined she must do whatever necessary to be present at its reading. Any document that affected people as strongly as it had the five guests gathered around the table was one certain to contain unexpected clauses – whether they had anything to do with the testator's death remained to be seen.

CHAPTER 4

After luncheon Evelyn took a book from the dusty shelves in the library and sat in an armchair as close to the fire as she dared. The cavernous room was, she decided, the coldest room in the house.

The old book smelled strongly of damp and when she opened it, she found many of the pages were stuck together. Hearing voices in the hallway, she quickly fanned the pages and made a show of being engrossed in the words.

She guessed, correctly, that if a will reading were to take place, the library would be the chosen venue. The police were in the library and Evelyn ensured her family were in the drawing room. Elise had arranged for a housemaid to light the fire. Although the girl had built a good fire, it had yet to warm the room.

"If we are not poisoned before the police allow us to leave, we shall all freeze to death if we are not careful," Louisa complained in a loud voice.

Evelyn did not look up from her book as Hugh's guests filed into the room. Edwin's was the next voice she heard. "Has anyone seen my attaché case? I'm certain I brought it down from my bedroom this morning. I intended on doing some work after luncheon, but I don't seem to be able to find it."

"You had it in the breakfast room this morning," Emma said helpfully. "No, no, you stay here. I shall run and find it for you."

"I thought my husband employed you as his secretary, girl?" Louisa asked scathingly. "It seems to me you spend as much time playing nursemaid to Mr Granville as you ever have working for poor Albert."

Evelyn forced herself to look at the book even though she'd much rather look at the people assembled in the room to see what their reactions were to Louisa's rudeness and Edwin's rather endearing habit of misplacing his belongings.

"Ah, Lady Northmoor." Peter Balfour shuffled his feet as he stood in front of her. "I didn't realise this room was occupied."

"Oh." Evelyn looked up and blinked rapidly, hoping her feigned surprise looked genuine. "I thought it would be nice to take my mind off the awful events by getting lost in a book. I'm afraid I rather took that to heart. This book is so engrossing I didn't even hear anyone come in."

"This is rather awkward." A faint blush stained Peter's cheeks.

"No it isn't," Louisa retorted. "Lady Northmoor, I'm sorry, but you need to leave."

"Leave?" Evelyn repeated. "But I understood the detective wanted us all to remain in the house."

"The room," Louisa snapped. "You need to leave the room."

"Oh dear," Evelyn said. "Has the detective commandeered the library, too?"

"We are to have a reading of my husband's will," Louisa said grandly.

"Oh, I see." Evelyn held up the book. "I'm rather enjoying

this book. Don't mind me, I shall just sit here and you won't even know I'm here."

A rather ugly look crossed Louisa's face, but she said no more as Emma came back into the room carrying Edwin's bag. "Let's just get on with it."

"As you wish." Peter moved away from Evelyn, so he stood in front of the little group of visitors. "Mr Lewis's last will and testament—"

"Where is it?" Louisa shrieked. "You can't read a will without having it in front of you."

Peter rubbed his eyes. "The thing is, Mrs Lewis, I don't have the will here with me."

"Then how do you intend to read it?"

"I should have made it clear earlier," he said, struggling to keep his composure. "I didn't know Mr Lewis would expire, and so I had no reason to bring his will with me to Rochester Park."

"Oh, for goodness's sake." Louisa swept out a hand. "What are we all doing in here, then? Why didn't you say something before now?"

"I know the will," Peter said. "That is, I can't read it verbatim, but Albert's is the only will I've ever drafted. I'm a business solicitor, so my specialism isn't in private law. I couldn't possibly recite the terms of conveyancing contracts because I have been involved in so many. But I can accurately recall each clause of Albert's will."

"Let's have it then!" Louisa actually tapped a foot in pure impatience. "You have made us wait quite long enough."

"Albert made some small bequests in his will. He leaves the sum of five hundred pounds to his loyal, long-serving and hard-working accountant, Edwin Granville."

"Oh. Oh, I say!" Edwin exclaimed. "How generous. I'm incredibly touched."

"He gifted one hundred pounds to his assistant Stanley Cameron with instructions that Mr Cameron should remain as manager of the business for at least one year. There are a few other personal items left to family members," Peter went on. "He leaves both his house in London and his home in Derbyshire to you, Mrs Lewis, for your use during your lifetime. In addition, he bequeaths the sum of ten thousand pounds to be paid to you on the last day of every year."

Evelyn gave up the pretence of reading the book in her lap as the glass ornament on the table next to Louisa's seat went sailing through the air and crashed into the wall above the fireplace. "I have been married to that man for years, and he leaves me only a paltry sum of money? That cannot be right."

"It's an extremely generous allowance." Peter lost his earlier nervousness and now seemed almost gleeful.

"But it's not everything, is it?"

"No," he agreed. "It isn't everything."

"Who gets the rest of it?" Louisa's gaze narrowed dangerously as she waited for the answer to her question.

"Mr Lewis's residual estate is bequeathed to Miss Emma Mountjoy."

"The secretary?" Louisa's voice was low but menacing. "He's left his entire estate to his secretary? Oh, this is too much."

"Those were your husband's wishes."

"Correct me if I am wrong, Balfour." Louisa stared at the floor where the shattered glass sparkled in the overhead light. "But the will allows me only to live in the houses, I don't own them. I receive a yearly sum of money and have no control over the business."

"That is correct. There is a specific clause in relation to the houses and property. You don't own any of it. You are not to sell any of the property. It is held in a trust and, after your death, passes to Miss Mountjoy."

"I assume I receive my first payment of ten thousand pounds at the end of this month?"

Evelyn could scarcely believe the change in Mrs Lewis. She was now icily calm, her words reasoned and considered.

"I will have to check how that clause is specifically worded, but yes, I believe that is right."

"Excellent." Mrs Lewis rubbed her hands together. "I shall use that money to engage a *competent* lawyer who will challenge the validity of this sham will all the way to the highest court in the land."

As quickly as Louisa's demeanour had changed, so did Peter Balfour's. His pleasant face hardened into a mask of fury. "I would advise you to rethink most carefully before you do that."

"Would you really?" Louisa's glare was full of disdain. "I shall not be taking any advice from you. What were you thinking drafting such nonsense?"

"I followed my client's instructions precisely." Peter returned Louisa's furious look with one of his own. "I can assure you that Mr Lewis was competent when he made the will. You have no grounds on which to challenge the document. It was drafted with the utmost care. The provisions made for you are extremely reasonable."

"I have given the best years of my life to that man, to our marriage." Louisa shook her head and her shoulders trembled. This time when she broke down, Evelyn had no doubt that her tears were real.

Emma Mountjoy used the distraction to get up and leave the room, the same rather guileful smile decorating her lips.

~

Tommy met with David and Hugh after the police had finished questioning everyone.

"It's very clear from the questions they asked me that the police believe I am the only person who could have accessed cyanide in the gardener's shed," Hugh said. "I ask you, is it really possible I was the only person who could have poisoned Albert?"

"As I pointed out during your interview," David said in his usual calm way, "you have absolutely no motive to kill Albert. In fact, out of everyone, you had the most to lose from his death. It seems highly unlikely that there will be any deal now that will help you financially."

"Is there anyone who has a motive?" Hugh asked.

"Evelyn has identified several." Tommy couldn't help his smile of pride. "Louisa inherits a yearly allowance following Albert's death. The big surprise is that Emma Mountjoy inherits the residual estate which, we can be certain, is considerable given the deal he was offering for the land here at Rochester Park. There is also something a little odd about Peter Balfour that you may be able to advise on, David."

"How can I help?"

"It was actually Aunt Em who realised that Peter may not be all that he seems."

David frowned. "In what way?"

"You'll understand this much better than I do. Apparently, when he referred to Mrs Lewis, he called her the 'executor' of Albert's will. Aunt Em is convinced that the correct term is executrix."

"Aunt Em is quite correct." David nodded. "However, I don't think you should read too much into the error. My understanding is that Balfour's practice is not in private law, so it isn't surprising he isn't au fait with the correct terminology."

"Really?" Tommy couldn't help the disbelief in his voice. "It seems an extraordinary mistake for him to make. If he didn't know what he was doing, he had no business drafting Lewis's will."

"That, of course, is another argument entirely."

"Is Balfour's competency something Mrs Lewis can call into question in court?"

"If I were acting on her behalf, I would call into question absolutely everything I could to get the validity of the will thrown out."

"She's an odious woman," Hugh commented, "but it doesn't seem right her husband left most of his estate to a mere secretary."

Tommy shrugged. "Perhaps that isn't all she was."

"I know it's jolly selfish," Hugh said, "but Lewis's death rather leaves me in a bit of a hole."

"You didn't want to sell out to him." David clapped a hand on Hugh's shoulder in a gesture of both comfort and support.

"I didn't, that's right." Hugh stared out of the window. "But we all know that was my only genuine option if I wanted to keep the house. Poor Elise. I never should have allowed her to convince me to marry her."

"Elise knew exactly what she was getting into." Tommy's mouth twisted wryly. "Do not underestimate her strength of character. The Christie women are made of sturdy stuff. She will stand by your side no matter what happens next."

Hugh swung his gaze back to Tommy. The despair Tommy saw there made him want to look away – the emotion was so raw. "Yes, she will. That is what makes me feel so desolate. The dear girl deserves so much better."

"Something will come along, old chap," David said, but with little enthusiasm.

They all knew Hugh's situation was dire. His family finances would not be shored up by selling a few paintings or pieces of antique furniture. How could Hugh's father have continued gambling knowing his recklessness was destroying his son's birthright?

"Might the Cameron fellow keep the deal on?" Tommy asked. "Perhaps everything isn't lost. Will you talk to him?"

"Wouldn't do any good." David shook his head sadly as he looked at Hugh with sympathy. "From what Evelyn told you, the will is very clear. Everything is left to Miss Mountjoy. That means any business decisions are now hers and Cameron's to make."

Hugh walked to the door. "I should speak to them both, see what their thoughts are. It isn't something I want to do, but I have little choice. At least I can see if the deal is still on the table."

"I wish there was more I could do," Tommy said as Hugh left the room. "I feel so terribly helpless."

"I've spent months trying to think of something that would help Hugh. Short of finding gold on his land, I can't think of anything that would rescue the situation. He's running out of time."

"Let's deal with the more pressing matter of Lewis's death first. That is, at least, something we can do for Hugh. Might you know someone in London that knows Balfour?"

David raised an eyebrow. "How is Balfour pertinent to the death of Albert Lewis?"

"I don't know," Tommy admitted. "Perhaps he had nothing to do with it. But Lewis was adamant he knew Mrs Balfour. I'd like to find out more about the Balfours if I can."

"I'll make a few telephone calls," David said. "Though it might be hard to get answers during the holidays."

"Nonsense," Tommy said briskly. "It means people will be home. Most men will probably be bored witless at having to spend enforced time with family and would be only too glad to have a few minutes' reprieve talking to you on the telephone."

"The instrument is in the main hallway." David looked at the door doubtfully. "It isn't exactly conducive for confidential telephone conversations."

"I understand there's a telephone line in the butler's room. Malton was quite insistent he would like me to install one downstairs at Hessleham Hall."

David laughed. "Will you?"

"If it meant never having to answer the infernal thing ever again, I just might. I know it's a jolly useful invention, but I miss the days when one heard the latest news by letter. So few people send letters these days."

"Well, I think the telephone is a wonderful invention," David said. "You're terribly old-fashioned, Tommy."

"I find it easier to express myself in a letter." Tommy remembered all too well back when he had written to Evelyn every day. Receiving a letter in return was the highlight of his day. He didn't think he would ever forget how much the simple correspondence had meant to him during the long war years.

"I shall make those calls." David got to his feet. "What shall you do next?"

"The police have nearly concluded their interviews," Tommy said grimly. "It is time for Evelyn and me to start ours."

~

*E*velyn hurried down the stairs to the kitchen. Detective Inspector Gregory had given everyone permission to move freely around the house, but she expected to be stopped before she got to the bottom of the stairs.

She glanced furtively behind her as she hurried along the corridor to the kitchen door. No one was there. However, a burly uniformed police officer was now stationed at the back door, arms crossed against his chest as he peered curiously in her direction.

"Lady Northmoor!" Mrs O'Connell jumped to her feet as Evelyn entered the kitchen. "I wasn't expecting to see you down here today. Not when there is sleuthing to be done."

"I know as well as you, Mrs O'Connell, that the heart of every house is its kitchen. Nothing goes on upstairs that the downstairs doesn't know about."

"Nora isn't here to tell you all the goings-on as she usually does." The cook poured a cup of tea for Evelyn and topped up her own cup. "Goodness knows I could do with the girl's help. This is the first chance I've had to sit down I've had since starting breakfast this morning. I don't mind admitting I'm fair tuckered out."

"Do you not have adequate staff numbers to help you?"

"It isn't that." Mrs O'Connell blew on her tea before taking a sip. "Nora and I have worked together for so long now she does what needs doing before I even think to tell her. The staff here can cope quite well with Lord and Lady Clifford in residence."

"They're not accustomed to dealing with dinner parties and overnight guests?"

"They're not." Cook leaned forward and lowered her voice. "It's fortunate Mrs Chapman thought to bring extra bed linen. The standard of cleanliness in some of the bedrooms was quite shameful."

"Perhaps they have become complacent."

Mrs O'Connell pursed her lips. "There's no excuse for laziness and, let me tell you, some of what goes on here is just sloppiness. None of us would stand for it at Hessleham Hall I can tell you."

"We shall have a meeting as soon as this business with poor Mr Lewis is concluded to discuss everything you and Mrs Chapman think is relevant."

Mrs O'Connell clicked her tongue. "Poor Mr Lewis? Begging your pardon, Lady Northmoor, but that man is not to be pitied. Did I hear correctly that he spilled his dessert in Lady Clifford's lap and then *laughed* about it?"

"He did." Evelyn took a sip of her tea. "Lady Clifford was frightfully upset."

"Disgraceful." The cook shook her head so vigorously the white cap swayed on its perch on top of hair that was decidedly more salt than pepper. "Now, I expect you want to know if we have found Mr Granville's lost cufflink?"

"Indeed, I do."

"As soon as I received your message from Doris, I instructed all the staff to be on the lookout." Cook glanced towards the kitchen door to be certain they were not being overheard. "The missing item was found on the floor in the dead man's room."

"Goodness me," Evelyn said. "How did the police miss that?"

A look of disgust settled on the cook's face. "Men never do know how to find what is usually underneath their very noses. The cufflink was on the floor near the bed. Granted, the eiderdown was covering it, but it's easy to lift that and search properly, isn't it?"

"It certainly is, Mrs O'Connell. Now, tell me, how can you be certain it is Mr Granville's cufflink?"

"Well, I can't be certain, of course," Mrs O'Connell said. "*I* haven't seen it, you understand. The girl who found it called on Mrs Chapman and she verified it was silver and monogrammed with Mr Granville's initials."

"And where is it now?"

The cook looked puzzled. "Why we left it where it was. Should we have moved it?"

Evelyn smiled. "No, no. That was quite the correct thing to do. We wouldn't want the police to think we were interfering, would we?"

"It can hardly be interfering if they cannot be bothered to do their job properly, can it? And to think they get paid to do something you and Lord Northmoor are so much better at."

"You're too kind." Evelyn sat back in her chair. "Now, is there anything else I should know?"

"Master Harry has a hip flask hidden under the handkerchiefs in his top drawer. Miss Grace has a romance book under her pillow. Nothing scandalous, a book quite suitable for a young lady, so I'm not sure why she doesn't have it out in plain sight."

"Perhaps she is embarrassed. Grace does not have her sister's confidence."

Mrs O'Connell grinned. "Ah, Miss Constance is leading young Lord Chesden a merry dance. She is a most sensible girl."

"What makes you say that?"

"It probably isn't for me to say." Mrs O'Connell seemed aware she might have said too much. Commenting on the family's relationships wasn't her business. "But as you've asked, I shall tell you what I know."

Evelyn took a sip of tea to hide her smile. She never doubted for one moment that Mrs O'Connell wouldn't share what she knew. "Please do."

"His man said last night that His Lordship is quite besotted by Miss Constance. He says he's never seen him like this before. Apparently, he is jolly keen but the young miss tells him only that she enjoys his company."

"Which no doubt drives a man like Lord Chesden to distraction. I'm certain he has never before met a girl who doesn't turn into a simpering fool around him." Evelyn laughed out loud. "Oh, well done, Constance!"

"She has a good head on her shoulders."

"Yes, she does." Evelyn smiled wistfully. "I'm afraid I wasn't as sensible as she is when it comes to matters of the heart. I couldn't string together a sentence when Lord Northmoor looked my way."

"If you don't mind me saying, it doesn't seem to have done you any harm, My Lady."

"I've certainly been very lucky." Evelyn got to her feet. "Thank you, Mrs O'Connell, you've been very helpful."

As she made her way back upstairs, Evelyn couldn't bring herself to regret speaking so honestly to Cook. No doubt others would think she was foolish to talk to her staff about personal matters, but she didn't see it that way. She genuinely liked her staff and found it difficult to remember to keep the expected boundaries between them. Their close relationship helped when she and Tommy were investigating crimes, as there was nothing her staff wouldn't tell her.

She hurried up the stairs with renewed vigour. There was so much to do.

Why did Albert Lewis think he recognised Clara Balfour? What was her husband hiding? Why had the businessman given away the bulk of his fortune to his secretary? And, most pressing, why was Edwin Granville's cufflink found in the dead man's bedroom – right next to where his body had lain?

CHAPTER 5

Tommy asked to speak with Edwin Granville in the billiard room. As they walked into the room, Edwin turned back to Tommy with a look of surprise on his face.

"Why, Northmoor, there isn't even a billiard table in this room. What on earth is going on here? This house and all the goings-on within it are, quite frankly, a bit much in my humble opinion. I think I shall telephone my son and ask him to collect me earlier than arranged."

"I don't suppose it has been the pleasant break that you were hoping for?"

Tommy walked over to a small table next to the window and sat in a chair. As he hoped, Edwin followed and sat opposite.

Once seated, he stared at Tommy as though he had gone quite mad. "That is an understatement. Albert Lewis, a man I greatly admired despite his character flaws, is dead. The man's secretary has inherited his sizeable estate. His wife, always an emotional creature at the best of times, seems to have completely lost her head. And to top it all off, you've brought me to this room calling it a billiard room and there is no table in here. Of course I want to go home."

"The room doesn't matter," Tommy said. "I was simply hoping to have a private conversation with you."

"Perhaps you should have just said so. I don't hold with you young people who don't say what they mean. Now, I wonder what I could have possibly done with my cheque book."

Tommy blinked at the sudden change in conversation. "Your cheque book? Why do you need that?"

"Bit of an impertinent question, Northmoor. But, if you must know, it's to write out a cheque to pay my son for taking me home, of course." Edwin spoke as though it was the most natural thing in the world for his son to expect payment.

"The police haven't yet released us, I'm afraid. We shall have to stay here until they do."

"I was rather looking forward to the shoot. I like to shoot. If that was rescheduled, I think I should like to stay."

Tommy's head ached. Talking to Edwin was worse than trying to hold a conversation with a distracted child. "That decision is in the hands of the police. I'm certain it depends on them solving Mr Lewis's murder."

"Jolly bad timing him dying like that. Spoiled all our fun." He patted the inside pocket of his jacket absent-mindedly. "Don't suppose you've seen my pen? It's silver, extremely good quality. I was certain I picked it up from my dresser this morning."

This time, Tommy was ready for the older man's ramblings. "I shall help you find it before you need to write the cheque. I'm also pleased to let you know we have found your cufflink."

The blustering stopped and a spark of what seemed like respect lit Edwin Granville's eyes. "Really? What wonderful luck. Where?"

"It was found next to Albert Lewis's body."

"But he died in his bedroom," Edwin said, any attempt at

commandeering the conversation with his incoherent mutterings over. "I've never been in the man's bedroom."

"*I* didn't think that you had."

Edwin tapped his nose. "But the police might think I have. I say, Northmoor, you were a jolly good sport not telling them. You *haven't* told them, have you?"

"I have not," Tommy confirmed. "Though I fear it is only a matter of time before they find it for themselves."

"You left it in there?" Edwin asked incredulously.

"Tampering with evidence is a serious offence." Tommy withdrew a packet of cigars from his pocket and offered it to Edwin. "Cigar?"

"How decent of you." Edwin withdrew a cigar and picked up a box of matches from the table. "I don't mind if I do. I always think it's incredibly civilised when a couple of chaps enjoy a smoke together."

Tommy accepted the matches from Edwin and lit his own cigar. He blew out a steady stream of smoke while contemplating his next words. "You do see why the cufflink has to stay where it was found?"

"I see that someone is trying to frame me for that heinous crime." Edwin pulled a heavy glass ashtray towards him and tapped a minuscule ash into it. "What I do not see is why someone would do that."

"Oh, I shouldn't think it's personal," Tommy said. "Rather, the murderer is simply trying to focus the police's attention away from themselves."

"It's likely to be that dreadful woman he married. Should've stayed single after his first wife died like I did. Not that any woman could have replaced my Enid. She was one of a kind. No, I have never met another woman since then that would tempt me back into matrimony."

He was rambling again. Tommy fought to find the right words to take back control. "I hadn't realised Mr Lewis was married before. What can you tell me about his first wife?"

Edwin chuckled. "She was a quite awful woman. Poor Albert had appalling taste. Very different to Louisa, though the marriage was no more successful. Gertrude was the one with the money. Perhaps she would've had a more pleasant countenance if she had a child, but alas, it wasn't to be. Albert had a number of lady friends before settling on Louisa because he believed she had connections that would increase his social standing."

"Was he incorrect in his assumptions?"

"Most definitely." Edwin laughed again. "Louisa was on a similar social stage as Albert. They both wanted to be invited to the best homes in the area and they each thought marriage to the other would bring that about."

Tommy leaned back in his chair, pleased the conversation was now flowing and he was finding out more about the victim. Granted, none of the information he was learning seemed remotely relevant to the crime, but he was content for now to learn what he could.

"How did they get it so wrong?"

"Louisa was from an old family, but they were quite poor. Rather like Lord Clifford. Though, of course, her people were not as grand. They had stopped being invited anywhere because it was clear all they wanted was to marry Louisa off to someone with money – *anyone* with money, actually."

"And so, she ended up being married to a man with pots of money but no chance of improving his social standing?"

Edwin nodded. "Exactly so. Though, it must be said, Louisa has worked very hard. She got herself on many committees since they moved to Derbyshire. It helped. Country people are not as snobby as town people."

"Why did they make the move from London?" Tommy asked. It seemed odd for a man so determined to make money and climb the social ladder to move away from the most important town in the land for both.

"A woman." Edwin blew out a steady stream of smoke. "I

understand Albert had got quite embroiled with this female, and Louisa got wind of it, and insisted they move away."

Tommy made his voice sound disinterested and void of the natural censure he felt when hearing about affairs. It didn't matter how universally accepted it seemed to be. To him, it was abhorrent. "How unusual for a wife to be so demanding."

"That's exactly what she is." Edwin shook his head. "Worst thing he did was pander to her whims back then, it only weakened his position going forward."

"How long ago was that?"

"Oh, some considerable time." Edwin stroked his chin thoughtfully. "Maybe twenty or so years."

"I understood it was more recent." Tommy frowned. "Didn't Balfour join Albert Lewis here only a short time ago?"

"Cameron ran things in London. He took his instructions from Albert, either via letter or the telephone. Occasionally Albert would go to London, but Louisa always insisted she go with him. It was more usual for Cameron and Balfour to come to Derbyshire for business. Eventually, I suppose Balfour's wife put her dainty little foot down and insisted they move here too."

"Hmm." Tommy tapped his cigar over the ashtray. "I spoke to Mrs Balfour at dinner last night. She didn't seem enthused about country life."

"Perhaps I misunderstood. Possible, of course, that I've got things wrong. I'm forever losing things, after all." He gave a self-deprecating laugh. "But when it comes to remembering conversations, I have complete recall. I'm certain it was Mrs Balfour who insisted on the move."

"What do you think about Mr Balfour?"

Edwin's eyes narrowed despite the casual tone of Tommy's voice. "He's a pleasant enough fellow."

"Competent?"

Edwin raised his eyebrows. "So far as I am aware. Why all the questions about Balfour?"

"I'm troubled by someone leaving your cufflink near Albert's body," Tommy said smoothly. "I'm simply trying to find out as much as I can about everyone else."

"Is everyone a suspect to you?"

"Yes," Tommy answered without a moment's hesitation.

"Even Lord Clifford?"

"Regrettably, yes." Tommy gave a quick nod. "It would be remiss of me not to include him, despite our friendship. One thing is for certain, Albert Lewis didn't kill himself, and that fact means I will not rest until I find the culprit."

Edwin stubbed out his cigar and rose. "Perhaps I shall stay a little longer after all. It might be rather fun to watch you ruffle some feathers during your investigation."

"You don't think the police have already done that?"

"Not at all." Edwin grinned. "Their questions were very tedious. I've told you much more than I told them."

"Why do you think that is?"

"Because you asked the right questions, I suppose." Edwin put out a hand. "I enjoyed our chat immensely."

Tommy accepted the handshake. "Likewise."

~

As Tommy was having his chat with Edwin Granville, Evelyn caught sight of Emma Mountjoy going into the library and hurried after her. Emma turned upon hearing Evelyn's footsteps.

"Lady Northmoor." Emma gave Evelyn a knowing look. "Are you looking for another book to read?"

"Not this time," Evelyn answered honestly. "I thought I might ask you a few questions about Mr Lewis's will, if you don't mind?"

"Ask me anything you like." Emma put her hands out, palms up. "I have nothing to hide."

"As a result of Mr Lewis's death, you're now an exceptionally rich woman. Is that correct?"

"I was only his secretary." Emma gave that small, secret smile Evelyn had noticed earlier. It wasn't quite sly, but it wasn't entirely pleasant, either. "I don't know enough about his business dealings to know how rich his death has made me."

"Were you expecting to be named in his will?"

"Oh yes." Emma sat in a chair next to the fire and held out her hands to the flames, then rubbed them together. "I always knew I would inherit."

"That's a strange way of putting it."

"I suppose it is."

Evelyn remembered Emma had told Tommy she was looking forward to the shoot. The direct route of questioning had not got her very far. Perhaps she would learn more by approaching things differently.

"My husband told me you were interested in my dogs?"

"That's a much safer topic of conversation, Lady Northmoor." That very distinct smile showed briefly on Emma's lips before she spoke again. "I should like to know more about your dogs. I'm not familiar with Gordon Setters."

"I would love to take you outside and show you the range of their skills, but it seems we are confined for the time being."

Emma appraised Evelyn. "I'm surprised the police haven't suggested using your dogs to see if they can pick up a scent on the footsteps outside on the lawn."

"It wouldn't do any good," Evelyn said. "Bloodhounds are exceptionally good at tracking but even they struggle in the snow. Something to do with the cold affecting the scent, I believe. My dogs wouldn't have a chance. Now, if there was a partridge in one of the bushes, they'd sniff that out extremely quickly."

"How fascinating," Emma replied. "So, there's really no way to know who those footsteps belong to?"

"I don't think so." Evelyn shook her head. "Ordinarily footprints can be matched to shoes, or boots. However, it seems whoever made the prints outside was aware of that and fresh snow was kicked over each impression."

"It seems we have a clever killer then?"

"They're all clever," Evelyn said drily. "Up until they say too much, or leave a clue they were not aware of, and are caught."

"I understand from Lady Clifford that you and Lord Northmoor have had some success in solving murders in the past. Do you think you will be able to unmask Albert's murderer?"

"We will do our very best," Evelyn replied. "No murder is pleasant but being poisoned is a particularly nasty way to die."

"Yes." Emma stared into the fire. "Poor Albert."

That was the second time she had referred to her employer as 'Albert' rather than the more appropriate 'Mr Lewis'. "It must have been terribly upsetting for you. Were you very close?"

"Of course," Emma answered without looking at Evelyn. "We worked together most days. I spent more time with him than his wife."

"Is that why he left you his money?" Evelyn asked. "Because he was fonder of you than his wife?"

"I should think so," Emma said plainly. "How could anyone have anything but contempt for the way Louisa Lewis conducts herself? All she cares about is money and social position. It doesn't make her a very likeable person."

"Are you yourself not interested at all in the money?"

"I didn't say that." Emma glanced at Evelyn, smiled, then

looked back into the flames. "The money will allow me to travel and have a very interesting life. I'm very grateful for the opportunities it will give me. However, Lady Northmoor, I did not kill Albert so I would get his money."

"I didn't—"

"No," Emma said softly. "You didn't ask me whether I had killed him, but that's ultimately what you want to know. That's why you're here talking to me now. It isn't because you thought it might be nice to get to know me. It's because you're trying to work out whether I am a murderess."

Evelyn laughed. It was so refreshing to speak to a young person who did not hide their personality behind a screen of fluffy conversation and non-committal sentences. "Yes, you're right. I'm sorry. I must seem incredibly rude to you."

"I feel as though I must tell you I can understand you are only doing your job." Emma gazed intently at Evelyn, her eyes seemed almost violet, as they calmly assessed Evelyn. "Except getting mixed up with murders is not your concern really, is it?"

"You mean it's none of my business," Evelyn retorted. "I can see why you would think that. Though you must see that if the police decide Lord Clifford is guilty of the murder, it will leave Lady Clifford quite bereft, and she is *family*. They may not have been married for long, but they are utterly devoted to each other."

"Is there nothing you won't do for your family?"

"Nothing," Evelyn said firmly.

"I can see that about you." Emma gave a brief nod before she looked away. "We are very similar in that way."

"You have family you would do anything to protect." It wasn't a question, but a statement Evelyn was certain was correct.

Emma didn't confirm the veracity of Evelyn's words. "There are things, and people, that are dear to each of us,

Lady Northmoor. How far we would go for love is as individual as each of us."

"What did Albert hold dear?"

"Money." Emma barked out a bitter laugh. "That always came first for him."

"Why?"

"Only someone who has an abundance of money, and always has had, could ask such a question."

"I'm afraid I don't know what you mean."

Emma crossed her long legs. "You were clearly born into privilege, Lady Northmoor. I was not. Neither was Albert."

Evelyn wanted to explain she had been a nobody before she married Tommy. She was just a girl from the village, but her parents were relatively wealthy. Tommy was a member of a rich and influential family but had never expected to inherit his title. That had only come about by a combination of the war, Spanish Flu, and murder.

To someone like Emma, who had to work for a living, Evelyn *was* privileged – before she had a title, and particularly afterwards. They were very different people. It usually wasn't so difficult for Evelyn to find common ground with whomever she spoke to. Emma Mountjoy was the exception – perhaps because the young woman was so very self-possessed.

"If I understand you correctly," Evelyn said carefully, "you say that Mr Lewis cared about money as much as he did because it gave him the security he had not had in his youth?"

"Yes." Emma lifted a shoulder. "I suppose you could put it like that. It also gives you choices that otherwise you would not have had. For example, I can now choose which shops I wish to patronise. I can decide whether I would like a Mediterranean holiday or whether I may like to go further afield. I might wish to go to the cinema on an evening, or I may prefer to go to London and watch a show."

"I suppose Mr Cameron will now run the business?" Evelyn wished she could take back the words as Emma's face darkened with consternation. She hurried to make amends for her thoughtless words. "Or will you choose to run *your* business yourself?"

"I may only be a secretary, Lady Northmoor, but I have learned enough about the business over the years I've worked for Albert to run it successfully."

"Of course." Evelyn licked her lips and took a moment to compose herself. She wasn't usually so clumsy when talking to people. "I apologise if I offended you. I certainly didn't mean to imply that you were not capable. The will didn't mention Mr Cameron, so I suppose I wondered what would become of him now."

"Mr Cameron has nothing to worry about, I am sure."

It was a strange answer and accompanied by that small smile that so unnerved Evelyn. She looked at Emma's hands – large, like the rest of her – and tried to imagine them taking apart Albert Lewis's blood pressure tablets, inserting cyanide, and then fastening the two parts together again. It didn't seem to fit Emma's personality as much as she knew of it.

Emma Mountjoy wasn't the type of girl to sit back and wait for something to happen. She seemed more the type to go out and get what she wanted and leave nothing to chance.

A thought occurred to Evelyn then – was it really possible that someone had time to put cyanide into *all* of Albert's tablets, or was it only those on top that had been disturbed? If all the tablets were affected, surely the murderer must be someone who had the opportunity to access the medication easily.

Emma got to her feet and Evelyn put away her thoughts. "It was nice talking to you, Miss Mountjoy."

"I shall see you at dinner, Lady Northmoor."

Evelyn waited until Emma had left the room before she got out of her own chair. The other woman made her feel uneasy, but not afraid. She also rather liked her – it was pleasant, though also a little discomforting, having a conversation with someone who didn't follow social conventions but instead chose her own distinct way of answering questions.

She felt as though she should warn Emma to be careful – but Evelyn wasn't sure if the girl would listen or even if her own apprehension was valid. How she hated this time when she didn't know who to trust and it seemed like they would never uncover the killer because, this time, they were too clever and had hidden themselves amongst the innocent too well.

~

Tommy caught Peter Balfour as soon as the police had finished with him. He led the man into the billiard room, and they sat in the chairs over by the window. The faint scent of cigars still lingered in the air, and Tommy wondered if it was too early to enjoy a brandy. Smoking and a tipple always went so well together.

"That was simply horrific." Peter ran a hand through his hair, rested his elbow on the arm of the chair, and dropped his chin into his upturned palm. "They asked me about all sorts of things. This deal, and that deal. Contracts I drew up years ago. I sometimes can't remember what I had for breakfast, let alone details of business that have long since been concluded."

"Do I understand that the police have someone in London going through Mr Lewis's files?"

"Oh yes," Peter said bitterly. "Going through everything, then questioning decisions Mr Lewis made through me. Did I know why he had called such-and-such a deal off? Was this fellow angry that Mr Lewis bought his company out from underneath him? How many people had threatened Mr Lewis? It went on and on."

"How very difficult for you," Tommy commiserated. "It sounds rather like you could do with a stiff drink to pep you up."

Peter raised his head. "What a splendid idea."

Tommy walked over to the drink cabinet in the opposite corner of the room and poured them both a drink – Peter Balfour's measure double his own. "Here we are. This should have you feeling more like yourself in no time."

Peter tipped back his head and emptied half the liquid. He then swirled what was left around the glass, as though trying to decide whether to drink it immediately or savour it. "I fear I made a mess of everything, Northmoor!"

Tommy leaned slightly forward. "What was there to get wrong? Surely you simply answered the detective's questions to the best of your ability, and that was an end to it?"

"You don't understand," Peter said miserably. "They twisted everything I said. By the end of it, they made it abundantly clear they thought I was incompetent, Mr Lewis was an unscrupulous rogue, and half of London wanted to kill him."

"Did he have a lot of enemies?"

"He wasn't always very pleasant." Peter sipped his drink. "So, there were many people who didn't like him, but whether any of those were upset enough to kill him is another matter entirely. There's a big difference between hating someone, and having enough anger to plan to kill them, then actually do it."

"That's very true," Tommy agreed. "And in this case, the murderer had lots of opportunities to change their mind. They decided Lewis's death was the only option, so they took his tablets, added the poison, then replaced the tablets. There were many distinct steps to take, so many chances to change their mind, and back out."

"I see what you mean." Peter regarded Tommy. "It's very different compared to shooting someone, or sticking a knife in, isn't it? Those are very immediate choices. Poison is premeditated."

"Oh, I think the other two methods can also be premeditated but, yes, they are more likely to be because of a sudden loss of control. There's nothing sudden about deciding to poison someone – it's very deliberate and takes a great deal of planning and execution."

"Yet it seems somewhat personal. Would an aggrieved businessman really come up to Derbyshire to poison Lewis's medication?"

"I wouldn't have thought so," Tommy answered. "If that is the angle the police are working, that it is more likely to have something to do with business, that is their lookout."

"But you will focus on a personal motive?" Peter asked, his earlier despair dissipating with each drop of brandy he consumed.

"It is too much of a coincidence, in my opinion, that he comes here and just happens to die from poisoning on the first night of his stay. Perhaps the murderer hoped the death would not be investigated thoroughly because it's the holidays. Maybe they struck as soon as they had an opportunity."

"But who could have knowledge of poison?" Peter finished his drink and looked longingly at the decanter across the room. "It doesn't seem to me that many people would know how to kill a person using cyanide."

"I'm not sure a person would have to be very skilled, or knowledgeable." Tommy frowned. "Most people understand that keeping potassium cyanide to kill wasps' nests, or vermin, is necessary but if consumed by humans, it is deadly."

Peter shuddered. "How perfectly dreadful. I can't imagine the nerve a murderer must have to kill that way."

"That is true." Tommy finished his own drink. "The murderer has not only gone in search of poison, but located it, brought it back into the house, got hold of Lewis's medication, et cetera, et cetera. It was very bold. They could have been discovered at any stage."

"Don't," Peter begged. "Don't let's talk about it anymore. I can't bear it."

Tommy wanted to ask the solicitor more – about his work for Albert Lewis, and the man's wife, but now didn't seem the time. The poor lawyer seemed close to having a breakdown, so extreme was his reaction to the police questioning.

Was that because he was a guilty man and trying desperately to hide it, or perhaps because he knew who the perpetrator was and was protecting them, or maybe it was another reason entirely. One that Tommy had not yet uncovered.

CHAPTER 6

*E*velyn went into the drawing room after she had finished speaking with Emma Mountjoy. She still felt somewhat unsettled after their conversation, though Evelyn believed preoccupation with Emma, and her secrets, would only prevent her from moving forward and closer to uncovering the murderer.

"Good afternoon, dear," Aunt Em said as she caught sight of Evelyn. "You're just in time for afternoon tea."

Evelyn looked around the room and gave a little frown. "Where is everyone?"

"The young people are all together in the music room. Constance is entertaining everyone by playing the piano." Aunt Em wrinkled her nose. "I came back in here for a little quiet and perhaps some civilised conversation. I'm not sure what tunes Constance was playing, but I'm certain it wasn't Mozart."

Evelyn exchanged a smile with Clara Balfour. No, it was unlikely that Constance was playing music that Aunt Em would recognise. The girl was as determined to stand out and be different as her sister was to blend in and do nothing which would invite attention.

"I will have a cup of tea with you, then I really must see how Mrs Lewis is."

Aunt Em held up a hand. "Sit down, dear. This is not your home, and Mrs Lewis is not your responsibility."

"But—"

"Lady Clifford has already spoken with Mrs Lewis. It is her intention to take tea in her room, though she said she may come down for dinner. She left strict instructions she does not wish to be disturbed and left poor Lady Clifford in no doubt as to who she thinks is responsible for her husband's death."

Evelyn accepted the gentle rebuke in the kindly way it had been intended.

"She is a most disagreeable woman," Clara said.

"Have you met her many times before?" Evelyn asked, keeping in mind Albert Lewis's assertion that he had seen Clara prior to arriving at Rochester Park.

"Yes," Clara confirmed. "On many occasions."

"Yet you had not met Albert Lewis before yesterday?"

"That is correct," Clara said. "Mrs Lewis and I are on several of the same committees. She is never one to agree with anything if she can find a contrary point of view."

"That must have led to some very tedious meetings."

Clara smiled and relief relaxed her pretty features. "Oh yes, Lady Northmoor. You cannot imagine."

"I think I can. Most committees have a similar personality, I believe. You simply cannot imagine the trouble my sister had with one such lady who insisted, in her esteemed opinion, we should not have a jam stand this year."

"Why ever not?" Clara asked with a chuckle.

"It turned out her strawberries had suffered with some sort of insect infestation and so she herself could not make her jam as usual. She was completely unable to see why anyone else should be allowed to exhibit their jam if she could not." Evelyn shook her head as she remembered Millie, her sister, trying insistently to move through the agenda for the meeting and the villager in question refusing to let the matter drop. "That simple meeting took over three hours!"

"Goodness," Clara said. "That sounds like a trial."

"What did you think of Mr Lewis?"

"I didn't really have much time to form an opinion about him," Clara said, not fooled for one moment by Evelyn's innocent sounding question. "As I said, I only met him for the first time yesterday."

"And yet he was quite insistent that he recognised you," Evelyn pressed. "Have you no idea where you could have come into contact with him before?"

"Obviously, we both lived in London before we moved to Derbyshire," Clara said. "And my husband worked for Mr Lewis, but I wasn't in the habit of meeting him at work. Peter and I like to keep work and home separate."

Evelyn frowned. "But your husband said very plainly at dinner last night that you often met him at work. Why would he say that if it wasn't true?"

Clara laughed – the sound high and nervous. She cleared her throat. "I'm afraid Peter was rather embarrassed on my behalf and told a little fib to divert Mr Lewis's attention away from me. He was rather intoxicated, wasn't he?"

"Yes, he was," Evelyn agreed, remembering how he had shortly thereafter upended his dessert in Elise's lap. Yet she couldn't help but feel that Clara had also tried to distract her from her own question. "Did you work when you lived in London?"

"Oh no, Lady Northmoor." Clara looked outraged, as though Evelyn had uttered a particularly foul word.

Evelyn tried to gauge how old Clara was. She could be anywhere from mid-twenties to mid-thirties. It really was so difficult to tell these days now so many more women were wearing face powder and rouge. "How long have you and Mr Balfour been married now?"

Clara looked taken aback by the question and, for a

moment, Evelyn thought she would refuse to answer. "Almost a year."

"Ah!" Aunt Em exclaimed. "Here's the tea. Wonderful. Just put it down there on the table, dear, and we shall pour for ourselves."

The young maid put the tea tray down and bobbed her knee before hurrying out. "Do you take milk and sugar, Mrs Balfour?"

"Milk, but no sugar, thank you." Clara Balfour put a hand on her midriff. "I find that sugar tends to upset my stomach."

"I do hope it isn't too tactless for me to congratulate you. What a wonderful anniversary present!" Evelyn passed Clara her drink.

The other woman smiled shyly. "I intimated to your husband last night that my condition is the reason I would not have attended the shoot today. I did not feel it prudent to go tramping over the countryside."

"Of course," Evelyn murmured. "Completely understandable."

"Is this your first marriage?" Aunt Em asked, then gave a small cough. "Do forgive an old lady for her inquisitive nature."

"So many questions!" Clara put her teacup down on the table beside her. Evelyn recognised both her words and the action for what they were – she was giving herself time to formulate an answer. "No, my first husband died."

"Oh, my dear, I'm so very sorry. I feel terrible for bringing up a painful subject."

Aunt Em did indeed look contrite. Clara Balfour, on the other hand, did not look at all perturbed. "It was many years ago now. I am quite over it. Peter is such a lovely man, a wonderful husband, that he almost makes me forget the past."

"Is it at all possible that Albert Lewis knew your first husband and you have simply forgotten you met him?"

Evelyn asked. "He did say that he thought your hair was different – as indeed it would be if you met him many years ago. Fashions change so frequently these days."

"I have said I never met the man before." Clara's demeanour changed, and she lost her calm, reasonable attitude. "I'm not sure how many more times I have to say it before you believe me. Albert Lewis was a crude and vulgar man. No doubt he has met many women in his life, but I categorically state, *again*, that one of them was not me."

The robust denial was somehow less believable than if Clara had simply asserted in a quiet, firm voice she was certain she had never met Albert Lewis prior to the previous day. Evelyn mentally noted that it would certainly be worth contacting Somerset House the following day, Wednesday, to find out who Clara Balfour's first husband was.

It was a peculiar facet of a murder investigation that some information appeared entirely unconnected to other knowledge – right until the pieces somehow slotted together in an unexpected, but whole, jigsaw, revealing the identity of the murderer.

~

Tommy bumped into Louisa Lewis as she descended the staircase before dinner that evening. He had stationed himself next to the Christmas tree in the hall and waited until she was halfway down the staircase before he walked past the tree, affecting what he hoped was a confused expression.

"Good evening, Mrs Lewis. I do hope you had a pleasant afternoon rest."

"Lord Northmoor," she acknowledged in a haughty voice. "Whatever are you doing loitering in the hall?"

"It seems my wife has mislaid her shawl." Tommy shrugged and looked hopelessly about. "Her puppies are often known for absconding with items of clothing. I saw the youngest puppy under the tree earlier and rather hoped he may have left the shawl there, but it appears I am out of luck."

"How curious." Louisa gave her head a little shake, as though she couldn't quite believe an earl would act in such a peculiar way and turned to walk towards the drawing room.

"Mrs Lewis, may I please beg a moment of your time?"

She turned and exhaled a slow, long-suffering breath. "If you intend to ask the same questions as the police, Lord Northmoor, I shall save you the time. No, I do not know who killed my Albert. Neither do I know why they did so. Though you could probably save yourself some time by going straight to that strumpet who worked for Albert. *She* is the one who inherits his fortune, so *she* must be the prime suspect."

"I suppose the police think your husband was having an affair with his secretary," Tommy said idly.

Louisa's dark eyes bore into him. "Albert was not a philanderer."

"Forgive me, Mrs Lewis," Tommy said in a conciliatory tone. "But I understood you moved to Derbyshire from London to get away from a particularly persistent lady friend of your husband's."

"Rumours," she snapped. "Some people can be so cruel. Or, perhaps, they are simply jealous. We moved to the country because we both prefer it here. Now, if that is all, I should like to have a drink before dinner."

Tommy held up his hand. "One more question, if you don't mind?"

"You may ask it," she said. "But I may choose not to answer it."

"Your husband was very insistent at dinner last night that he had met Mrs Balfour before. Do you have any inkling where they could have met?"

"Are you suggesting that she was the person involved in the scurrilous rumours about Albert's faithlessness?"

"No, absolutely not." Tommy smiled, took a step closer, and patted Mrs Lewis's arm. "Obviously your husband died shortly—"

"Was killed, Lord Northmoor!" she cried out and, for the first time, Tommy sensed genuine pain from the widow. "My Albert didn't simply keel over and die from natural causes. Someone deliberately, and cold-bloodedly, murdered him!"

"You are quite correct," he said. "Please accept my apologies for my thoughtlessness. You have been through a quite dreadful ordeal. My intent is only to try and help you reach a kind of peace where your husband's murderer is apprehended, and you can at least have a sense of justice following your loss."

"I don't know the woman. *I* have never seen her before. She's the sort one isn't likely to forget, isn't she?"

"Yes," Tommy agreed. "She is very striking. Perhaps that's what made your husband so adamant that he recognised her – once seen, never forgotten."

"Now if you don't mind, I—"

"Sorry, Mrs Lewis, one more thought occurs to me." He put a hand on her elbow. "If your husband was not having an affair with Miss Mountjoy, do you know the reason he left the majority of his fortune to her?"

"There is only one possible explanation as far as I can see," she said, her voice weary, as though all the fight had gone out of her.

"And that is?"

"Clearly Albert had gone stark raving mad." Her eyes flashed. "Utterly bloody berserk, Lord Northmoor!"

∽

*E*velyn had spoken to Elise in advance and ensured that she sat next to Stanley Cameron during dinner. To her surprise, she found Albert Lewis's manager to be a gregarious and rather fun dinner companion.

He was a large man – over six feet tall and built like a country farmer. His shoulders seemed almost as wide as the doorways. However, he ate carefully and did not bump or jostle her with his elbows. She supposed he had spent years becoming accustomed to his size and learning to manage it in relatively confined spaces.

"I expect you will continue to run Mr Lewis's company on behalf of Miss Mountjoy?" she enquired.

Stanley glanced across the table to where Emma Mountjoy sat before answering. "For so long as it pleases Miss Mountjoy. She is, after all, the owner now. I work at her pleasure."

Evelyn felt Emma's eyes on her and looked up from the excellent carrot and parsnip soup. That odd smile – the one that told of a secret only Emma knew – was on her lips once more. She turned back to Stanley. "May I ask, Mr Cameron, are you happy to work for a woman? Although we now live in more enlightened times, I am aware some men would see it as beneath them."

"If I am doing work that I enjoy, I care not who pays my wages, Lady Northmoor."

"*Do* you enjoy your work?"

"Very much." Stanley finished his soup and carefully laid down his spoon.

"I understand Mr Lewis was not always easy to work for."

"Mr Lewis had certain peculiarities but, as I worked for him for many years, I was accustomed to them." His voice, though carefully modulated, told of his London roots.

"I hope you do not think I'm being impertinent," Evelyn said. "You say you worked for Mr Lewis for a long time. Do you mind telling me for how long?"

"I've worked for him almost since the start," Stanley said proudly. "Back then, I was a cheeky young chap, and one day I asked him if he could spare a couple of pennies. He said he could, but I had to earn them. I delivered messages, letters, documents, whatever he needed all over London. At first, I suspect he gave me things of little importance, but as he grew to trust me, I stopped delivering messages and started attending meetings with him."

"He must have respected you immensely."

"I like to think he did, Lady Northmoor." Stanley smiled and seemed lost in his memories for a moment. "I certainly respected him."

"It sounds a little like you were friends," Evelyn ventured.

"Oh, I wouldn't go that far." Stanley shook his head. "We didn't mix socially. In fact, my attendance here at Rochester Park is the first time I have been at the same social event as Mr Lewis. I was very much his apprentice."

"And now, it seems, you are to be the master."

"I suppose I am." He rubbed his hands on his trousers, then seemed to realise what he was doing and took a drink of wine. The delicate glass looked small in his huge hands. "At least so far as Miss Mountjoy allows."

"Have you enjoyed a cordial relationship with Miss Mountjoy?"

He frowned. "What do you mean?"

The suspicion in his voice seemed out of place for what Evelyn thought of as an innocent question. She clarified her intent. "You have worked alongside Mr Lewis, and therefore Miss Mountjoy, for a length of time. I simply wondered if you had a pleasant relationship and could therefore hope that would continue as you move forward in your new roles."

"Oh. Oh, yes, I see." Stanley nodded, seemingly relieved. "She is a very pleasant young woman."

Evelyn noted he repeated a word she used rather than chose one of his own. Was that because he didn't really know how to describe Emma Mountjoy or, as Evelyn suspected, he perhaps harboured some romantic feelings towards Emma?

"You must be the person who was closest to Mr Lewis, apart from his wife. That must give you a unique insight into the people in his life and, perhaps, those most likely to want him dead."

Stanley looked alarmed, and he again glanced across the table at Emma before answering. "Peter Balfour is too nervous to have killed Mr Lewis. I think it would have taken a man of real courage to murder him. The risks he took getting the poison! Definitely not a crime Balfour could have pulled off. As for poor old Granville, he would have misplaced the poison at least three times before using it."

Evelyn laughed, as she was sure Stanley intended, at his accurate description. The accountant seemed to have an unfortunate knack for losing his possessions on a regular basis. "He seems a harmless fellow."

"Not quite as dotty as he appears though, I don't think."

"Really?" Evelyn hoped she didn't sound too eager. "How so?"

"Mathematics isn't my strongest skill and, of course, Mr Granville was employed for his expertise in that area, but I'm certain money was missing from Mr Lewis's business account." Stanley looked around as though wary of being overheard.

"You say you're certain?" Evelyn asked carefully. "How can you be certain?"

"I have an exceedingly good memory." Stanley bent low over his empty bowl, so he was not overheard. "I remember the exact amount of money involved in deals I helped negotiate. Probably because it's not my money, so I am more meticulous about how it is spent. It seems to me that the figures reported in the accounts are incorrect."

"You suspect this money is being embezzled?" Evelyn couldn't keep the shock from her voice. As Mrs O'Connell would crudely put it, Edwin Granville didn't appear to be the sort of man who could find his backside with both hands.

"If he wrote the correct figures into the income column and misappropriated the money in the expenditure section, I would be none the wiser. I couldn't hope to see money vanishing in that way. However, I remember the amount involved in deals and that has frequently been entered wrongly."

"Is Miss Mountjoy aware of your concerns?"

"I shared my worries with her some weeks ago," he confirmed. "It is Emma who spent hours verifying my suspicions."

He flushed a little as he referred to the secretary using her Christian name. Evelyn pretended she had not noticed his slip-up. "Were either of you intending to tell Mr Lewis?"

"Indeed, we were," Stanley said. "We thought after the festivities of the season. It was our intention to speak to Mr Lewis together in the new year."

"Does Mr Granville suspect you're aware of his duplicity?"

"We don't think so." Stanley's face took on a worried look. "Then Mr Lewis was killed. Perhaps I am to be next because of the knowledge I have."

Evelyn eyed him shrewdly. "You're not talking about Mr Granville now, are you?"

"I am not," Stanley confirmed. "I am taking a chance telling you this information, but I feel I must. If something happens to me, at least I will have shared what I know with another person."

"Did you not think to tell the police?"

"No." Stanley screwed up his face as though he had eaten something repugnant. "They treated me as though I was still an apprentice and of no more worth to Mr Lewis than an office boy who is not trusted to do anything but brew a pot of tea."

"I do find that sometimes the police can only see what is directly in front of them and so do not look any further."

"That is exactly it." Stanley leaned a little closer to Evelyn. "I'm afraid that if I told them what I know, it would be the worse for your friend Lord Clifford. The police already believe him to be the culprit on account of this being his house and all."

Stanley's cockney accent became more pronounced as he became more eager to tell Evelyn what he knew. "I must admit that I got that impression from them too."

"Mr Lewis spoke to Lord Clifford before dinner last night," Stanley confessed. "About the deal he offered for Lord Clifford's land."

"Did he?" Evelyn was confused. She wasn't aware from anything Hugh had said to Tommy that he had a conversation with Albert prior to his death.

"Mr Lewis told Lord Clifford he didn't want to do business with him."

Poor Hugh. Perhaps that was why he had said nothing – his one chance at saving his family home was gone.

"I didn't know that."

"I was there." Stanley looked down at the tablecloth, embarrassment staining his cheeks. "Mr Lewis was rather rude to Lord Clifford."

"What did he say?" Evelyn couldn't keep the sharp tone from her voice.

"He said he never really intended to buy land on the estate."

"He didn't? Why was he here then? That makes no sense."

Stanley hesitated, and Evelyn's heart thundered behind her ribs. "He was here to have dinner at a grand manor house. With three earls, no less! He was bragging about that in the office for weeks. Once he heard Lord Clifford was friends with Lord Chesden, and then you were also invited for Christmas, he concocted a reason to do business with Lord Clifford and finagle an invitation."

"That's perfectly dreadful," Evelyn said heartily. "Did he tell Lord Clifford his reasons? His exact reasons, as you have so clearly explained?"

"I'm afraid he did, Lady Northmoor." Stanley sounded incredibly upset and his face betrayed his intense embarrassment. "Lord Clifford looked extremely distressed."

"I thank you for telling me," she said. "It was decent of you. I'm sure my husband will speak to Lord Clifford. If he hasn't already told the police, he must."

"Oh no," Stanley said, desperation causing him to forget to lower his voice. "If he does, it'll surely be the hangman's noose for him."

"Do hush," she admonished. "The police cannot charge him with a crime I am certain he hasn't committed despite his anger at Mr Lewis."

"Who else could it have been?" Stanley asked plaintively.

Who else, indeed?

It was true that Stanley's revelations now cast Hugh in the role of most likely murderer, especially if he hadn't shared the details of his last conversation with Albert to the police. Such explosive revelations were so rarely kept secret.

Evelyn looked up and saw Alexander Ryder looking directly at her, one eyebrow cocked questioningly. She remembered Aunt Em declaring with certainty that Alex would do anything for his family – did that extend to his very dear friends? Would Alex, had he known about Albert pulling out of the deal, have exacted revenge on the businessman?

She didn't doubt that he had the guts to perform such a dastardly crime. Just as Stanley said, she too believed that the killing of Albert Lewis required someone with incredible bravery. For Constance's sake, she hoped that person wasn't the man who she had pinned her heart, and dreams, upon.

CHAPTER 7

"You must see how this looks?" Hugh's despair was clear to see, but this was no time to leave things unsaid.

"I know." Hugh sat down heavily on an ancient carved mahogany sofa in the library that looked about as comfortable as a church pew. "I do know, but I barely had time to process what Lewis said to me before he was dead."

"Cameron said he never intended to do business with you. It was all a cruel ruse," Evelyn said quietly.

"Yes." Hugh dropped his head into his hands. "And like a fool, I fell for it."

"Where were you after dinner?" Tommy asked. "Specifically after Elise went up to bed? She said you were to follow behind her, but you didn't. Where did you go?"

"In here," he said morosely. "I couldn't bear to see Elise's disappointment when I told her Lewis would not save us from losing the house and the shame of bankruptcy."

"I think the police are a bigger problem than Elise right now." Tommy paced in front of Hugh. "How long do you think you've got before they know about Lewis's nastiness and decide you killed him? They already think you're the most likely candidate because it's your house and you would know better than anyone else where to find the cyanide."

"That's ridiculous, Tommy, you know it is!" Hugh lifted tired eyes to look at Tommy. "Do you know what your gardener keeps in his shed at Hessleham Hall?"

"Of course not," Tommy admitted.

"It's pointless going over what should have been done, who knew what, and why Lewis behaved as he did," Evelyn said reasonably. "The question is: what are we going to do about it now?"

"I think you need to tell the police everything," Tommy said. "Before someone else does. It'll sound much better coming from you."

"I can't do that." Hugh shook his head vehemently. "I'll be arrested on the spot. When Father died, I thought things couldn't get any worse, but look how wrong I was. Not only will I lose Rochester Park, but I may well lose my life."

"Pull yourself together!" Tommy's voice was sharper than he meant it to be. "Did you kill him?"

"Of course not!"

"Then the police can't find evidence you did, can they?" he said reasonably.

"Unless the actual murderer decides to frame me to divert attention away from themselves."

Tommy had no argument to refute Hugh's assertion. That was a genuine possibility. In fact, if Lewis's killer was clever, that was exactly what they would do. What better way to appear innocent than the obvious guilt of someone else?

"Don't you trust me?"

"You know I do, Tommy, you have been a great friend to me."

"Then tell me the truth. Everything you know. Expecting Evelyn and me to unmask a killer when you're hiding things from us is as difficult as juggling with one hand tied behind our back. You must see that?"

"I can see it now," Hugh accepted. "At the time I was struggling to accept everything that happened – Lewis withdrawing his offer, his carelessness at dinner, and the way he laughed at Elise's distress. I was trying to hold my anger in, not plotting how to kill Albert!"

"After dinner, you were with the other gentlemen in the dining room, or in the drawing room, until everyone retired to bed. Is that correct?" Evelyn asked.

"Yes. I came in here instead of going to bed."

"How long were you in here for before you heard the commotion upstairs?"

"Perhaps ten minutes or so." Hugh frowned. "I don't understand what you're getting at. Does this help me?"

"Immensely," Evelyn confirmed. "If Lewis only told you immediately before dinner that he was pulling out of the deal, and your movements are accounted for until approximately ten minutes before he died then when would you have had the opportunity to get the cyanide, and add it to Lewis's tablets?"

Hugh brightened, and he sat up straighter. "Does that prove I didn't do it?"

"Not exactly." Tommy stopped pacing and Hugh's shoulders slumped. "It means that when you had a motive to kill him, you didn't have the opportunity."

"But I had opportunity earlier in the day, didn't I?" Hugh tapped a foot on the floor. "But why would I want to kill him when I thought his money would save Rochester Park?"

"That is the logical argument and one I hope the police will listen to."

"Oh, not that again." Hugh got to his feet, his agitation ramping up a notch. "You can't mean for me to speak to them. You simply can't."

"I am afraid that you must," Tommy said reasonably. "I really believe it is for the best."

Hugh turned to Evelyn. "What do you think?"

"People talk. I agree with Tommy that it is only a matter of time before the police know what we know. They may take your economy with the truth as evidence of your guilt."

"If you both think that is the best thing for me to do, then I shall do it." Hugh nodded firmly to confirm his decision. "I shall talk to Elise at once, then go to Detective Inspector Gregory."

"I'll get David, he should go with you." Tommy reached out a hand and patted Hugh on the back. "It will be alright, old fellow, you'll see. You're doing the right thing."

~

While Tommy and David went with Hugh to speak to the police, Evelyn went down to the kitchen.

Mrs O'Connell was sitting at the huge wooden table with a pot of tea next to her and her swollen ankles propped up on a stool. "Lady Northmoor, I'm so glad you received my message before you retired for the evening."

"You look quite exhausted, Mrs O'Connell." Evelyn examined the cook's pale face and the dark smudges underneath her eyes.

"I am, My Lady. It's been a busy couple of days." She crossed her arms underneath her ample bosom. "Things will be easier tomorrow."

Evelyn looked doubtfully around the kitchen, which was still a hive of activity despite the late hour. "Will it really?"

"Lady Clifford has discussed a simple menu tomorrow evening. I don't mind telling you, I'm awfully glad. Being on my feet as much as I have been the last two days is getting harder at my age." She slapped a hand on the table. "But you're not here to listen to my woes."

"I am worried about you," Evelyn said quietly. "I'm afraid it was rather selfish of me to bring my staff down here and expect things to be exactly as they are at Hessleham Hall."

"Not at all, My Lady." Mrs O'Connell poured a cup of tea and slid it across the table to Evelyn. "You were not to know that most of the staff here have never catered to such a large group. Perhaps if—"

"You miss Nora," Evelyn interrupted. "I can see that. Not just because of hard work."

"I do." Cook sighed. "I might tell her off for prattling on sometimes but having her around lightens my load in more ways than one I can tell you."

"I suppose it must be like how I feel about Miss Constance." Evelyn smiled. "Sometimes she makes my head ache with her youthful exuberance, and her constant cheerfulness, but goodness, she's fun to be around even if she makes me feel at least eighty!"

"Yes, My Lady, that's exactly it." She sipped her tea. "You're always so understanding."

"I need you to do something for me." Evelyn blew across the top of her tea. "I will come back down to the kitchen at precisely eleven tomorrow. I expect to see you resting and the staff Elise employs doing exactly what you have told them to. You must stop trying to do everything yourself."

"Oh but, My Lady!"

"No buts," Evelyn said firmly. "I insist, and I know Elise will agree with me. I'm certain she will speak to her staff in the morning. I simply can't have you going back to Hessleham Hall too tired to enjoy being back with Nora."

"Thank you." Cook accepted the directive meekly, but it did not fool Evelyn. Mrs O'Connell would still be up before anyone else in the morning, determined that breakfast would be as perfect as every other meal she was to make.

"Now, you sent for me. What do you have to tell me?"

"Mrs Chapman reports it is quite apparent from Miss Emma Mountjoy's bedroom that she does not spend the nights alone." The cook glanced at Evelyn. "I'm desperately sorry if that shocks you, My Lady."

Evelyn waved a dismissive hand. "I think we both know I have seen and heard of worse behaviour. I'm quite certain I know the gentleman involved."

Mrs O'Connell added another heaped teaspoon of sugar to her cup, poured more tea and added a dash of milk. She gave the liquid a stir before continuing. "The other matter, I fear, will be of more concern."

Evelyn sat forwards wondering what the cook would tell her. Could she be told anything that would shock her? Over the last couple of years, she was certain the things she had seen and heard of people doing had rendered her quite impossible to surprise.

"Oh dear. Has this information come from Mrs Chapman too?"

"One of the housemaids told her. The girl was very distressed."

"I'm sorry to hear that. What did she tell Mrs Chapman?"

"There's a vase missing from the library." The cook held up a hand as Evelyn was about to speak. "I know what you'll say. You will say that perhaps someone has broken it and hidden the evidence, so they don't get into trouble. Maybe Elise has moved it somewhere else. There are lots of explanations, but Mrs Chapman has exhausted them with the staff. The vase has vanished into thin air."

Evelyn didn't want to be dismissive, but this hardly seemed like important news. "Was it a vase Elise is particularly fond of?"

Mrs O'Connell smothered a laugh. "Lady Clifford has a very eloquent turn of phrase, as you know. Apparently, she described it as 'the foulest thing I have ever had the misfortune to set my eyes upon – it's the exact colour of pond scum and about as welcome in my house'. Those were her very words."

Evelyn smiled. "I'm sure. Yet it stayed in the house, obviously. She didn't get her wish and have it banished."

"Lord Clifford evidently put his foot down. He insisted it had to stay on account of the fact it is a family heirloom and exceedingly expensive."

"Does Mrs Chapman think someone has stolen it because of its value?"

"There are rather a lot of people in the house, and we don't know them. Any of them could be a thief and we wouldn't know. After all, one of them is a murderer."

That was certainly true, but another, more worrying thought had occurred to Evelyn. Was it possible the vase was insured, and Hugh had arranged for its disappearance himself so he could claim the insurance money? She didn't think it was likely – any money he would receive for the valuable item wouldn't put much of a dent in Hugh's debts. However, it was certainly a curious turn of events.

"I will have to tell Lady Clifford, of course." Evelyn sipped her hot tea. "I wish I didn't have to. She has enough on her mind at the moment without having another thing to worry about."

"That is precisely how I felt about the situation," Cook confided. "But I knew the best thing I could do was tell you. I have confidence you will know exactly what to do."

"You certainly have more faith in me than I have in myself."

"What will you do about the other matter?"

"I don't think I can do anything." Evelyn lifted a shoulder in a gesture of surrender. "It is Miss Mountjoy's personal business. It's possible it is linked to the investigation, so I am glad I have that knowledge. Please thank Mrs Chapman for passing it on."

At that moment, the dinner gong sounded loudly and persistently as though someone was striking it with as much force and frequency as they could.

Mrs O'Connell jumped to her feet to get a washcloth to mop up the tea she had spilled on the table. She clutched her chest. "I can't remember the last time I had such a fright!"

Evelyn reached out a hand and rested it on the cook's arm. "Are you alright?"

"Yes, My Lady, it was just the shock. I assure you I am quite well."

"Remember what I said about the rest." Evelyn hurried to the door, then turned back and pointed a finger towards the cook. "I meant what I said. I shall be here at eleven tomorrow to ensure you are taking an extended break."

"Yes, My Lady." She bobbed her head.

Reluctantly, Evelyn raced up the stairs as quickly as she dared, so she could see what was happening in the hall.

~

Tommy walked over to Evelyn as she appeared at the top of the servants' stairway. "There you are. I really wish you had told me where you were going off to, darling. I was becoming quite afraid for your safety."

Evelyn met his gaze steadily. "I told you Mrs O'Connell wished to see me."

He caught hold of her hand and gave it a slight squeeze. "I didn't know you were going then. Detective Inspector Gregory wants us all together in the drawing room."

"Was that the reason for the over enthusiastic gong banging?"

Tommy grinned, his fear forgotten now he could see Evelyn was safe. "It was quite amusing. The Detective Sergeant hit the gong quite satisfactorily, but Detective

Inspector Gregory was not satisfied. He insisted the sergeant go at it again 'with all he had'."

"I heard it all the way down in the kitchen," Evelyn said. "It gave poor Cook quite a fright."

"Did she have lots to tell you?" Tommy whispered as they walked into the drawing room.

Evelyn was prevented from answering as the detective glared their way. "Ah, Lady Northmoor. We have been waiting for you. May I ask where you've been?"

"You may ask," she said in a voice so imperious she sounded exactly like Aunt Em.

He frowned at her response, waited for her to answer his question, then seemed to realise she didn't intend to say any more. "Where were you?"

"You said we were to stay inside the house," Evelyn replied. "That is where I have been. I see no reason to give you any further details."

His face reddened, and he opened his mouth, then closed it again as though he thought better of whatever he was going to say. He turned back to the expectant faces of the family and guests gathered together at his behest. "I said I would talk to you all again when I had more to report. Following the conclusion of our interviews, we became aware of new information this evening which we must treat with the utmost urgency. Lord Clifford, I must ask you to accompany me to the police station in Derby for further questioning."

"That can't be right!" Elise cried. "Hugh came to you himself with the information!"

"Lady Clifford, please," the detective said in a voice heavy with condescension. "Please don't make this any harder than it needs to be."

"I say." David got to his feet and moved forward to stand next to Hugh. "I don't see any reason the further questions you have can't be put to Lord Clifford here in the house."

"It is our prerogative to question suspects whenever and

wherever we choose," the detective replied haughtily. "We are not obliged to give Lord Clifford consideration that we wouldn't offer any other suspect."

"I insist on—"

"Yes, yes, Mr Ryder. Lord Clifford has a right to have his solicitor present." The detective motioned to a uniformed officer, who removed his handcuffs from his belt and walked over to Hugh. "Lord Clifford will travel to the police station in one of our cars. You can make your own way there."

"By myself?" David lifted an eyebrow. "Am I not a suspect?"

"I suppose you will have to travel with us," the detective said unenthusiastically.

"Must you cuff him?" Alexander Ryder moved to stand next to his friend. "Is that really necessary?"

"He is a murder suspect, Lord Chesden." Detective Inspector Gregory nodded at the uniformed officer who fastened the handcuffs onto Hugh's wrists. "In my opinion, it would be foolhardy if I didn't secure a prisoner on the journey to the police station."

Hugh turned a sorrowful gaze on Elise. "I'm so sorry, my darling."

She rushed forward and clutched his hands in her own. "You have nothing to be sorry for. You have done nothing wrong. It is only a matter of time before this unintelligent buffoon realises his supremely ridiculous error."

"When you get him to the station," Louisa Lewis said in a loud voice edged with forced boredom, "be sure to throw away the key."

"I wish I could remember more about that night," Constance said morosely. "If only I could be sure about what I saw and heard, then I'm certain you would know that Hugh could not possibly be the murderer!"

"Do not fret." Alex smiled gently at Constance, then got to his feet and put a hand on the detective's arm, his voice low and menacing. "Lady Clifford is right. You are making a terrible mistake."

"Take your hand off me," Detective Inspector Gregory snapped. "Otherwise, you will accompany us to the station on charges of impeding a police officer in his lawful duties. Step back, Lord Chesden!"

"Now is not the time for heroics, Alex," David said. "Let us not make things any more difficult for Lord and Lady Clifford."

Alex stepped back and dropped his hands to his side, but his furiously scorching glare did not leave Detective Inspector Gregory's face. Not for the first time, Tommy thought this was not a man it would be wise to cross. Was he right in allowing a man who obviously burned with such anger to court his baby sister?

"Take him away," the detective said with unnecessary fervour. He waited until they had led Hugh from the room before again facing the stunned group. "This afternoon I received a report from an officer who visited Rochester Park's former gardener. He confirmed the amount of cyanide in the shed when he left his employment here. I can now state with certainty that there is a significant quantity of the poison missing."

"Didn't we already know that?" Tommy asked.

"We strongly suspected that was the case," the detective said smoothly. "Now we have a written statement from the gardener. We therefore conclude the cyanide taken from the shed was used to poison Mr Albert Lewis, leading to his untimely death."

"I have some advice for you, Detective Inspector," Aunt Em said loudly. She waited until he looked her way before continuing. "Do not contemplate changing your career to one on the stage. Your acting is appallingly amateur and, quite frankly, in terrible taste."

"I am setting out the police case against Lord Clifford."

"Nonsense," snapped Aunt Em. "You are telling us nothing that we didn't already know. What you are currently doing is grandstanding and it neither enhances your 'evidence' nor our opinions as to your competency."

Wisely, Detective Inspector Gregory left the room, saying no more.

CHAPTER 8

As soon as the police left the room with Hugh, David hurried Evelyn and Tommy into the library. Alex looked as though he wanted to follow but, at the last moment, he seemed to realise that he had promised to stay with the Christie family. He looked longingly after them, clearly wishing to be involved in the case more rather than on the fringes doing what amounted to glorified babysitting duty.

"Shouldn't you be with the police?" Tommy asked, frustration making his voice harsher than normal.

He felt guilty, that much was obvious. He had persuaded Hugh to speak to the police, and it had ended with him being arrested!

"Apparently they need a little time to settle Hugh in the police car, whatever that means," David said. "I don't know how long I shall be gone so I wanted to share a little information I have learned with you before I left."

"Let us hope it is helpful," Evelyn murmured.

"I don't know if it is," David replied. "All I can do is tell you both and leave the knowledge in your hands while I do what I can for Hugh at the police station."

"Tommy, do sit down!" Evelyn implored. "You make me

quite nervous when you stalk up and down like a wild animal."

"It makes me nervous to sit still," Tommy retorted. "At least if I'm moving, I feel like I'm doing *something*. I feel so very helpless. And, of course, responsible that Hugh has been taken away in handcuffs. I should never have—"

"Oh balderdash! Stop talking about things we cannot change and let's hear what David has to tell us."

"As I've said, it's not very much." David sat on the uncomfortable-looking Sheraton sofa and crossed his legs. "I made a few phone calls earlier today. The result being no one I have spoken to went to university with Peter Balfour. Now, this isn't as strange as you might think. Many people entered the legal profession as articled clerks—their time may, or may not, have been interrupted by service during the war."

"Can we find out if he was an articled clerk?" Evelyn asked.

"We can, but we would have to know who he was articled to."

Tommy, who had stopped pacing, now strode across the rug, then turned and marched back. He caught sight of Evelyn's face. "I'm sorry, darling. I can't help myself. Somehow, the movement helps me to think better. Does it matter if we know who he was articled to?"

"It will help us know whether he is a qualified solicitor," David said.

"Yes, I understand that. I'm trying to work out in my mind whether it matters. To the case, I mean."

"The law is the sort of profession where people know each other, isn't it?" Evelyn asked. "I wouldn't expect a country solicitor in Derbyshire to be known in London but if that country solicitor had worked for years in London, then it stands to reason that he would have trained with other lawyers, and *someone* would know where he was articled if not with whom."

"That's definitely true, though you must remember I have only spoken to a few chums. Perhaps we will have more luck tomorrow in finding out more when people go back to work."

"I think it's necessary to find out as much about both Peter and Clara Balfour as we can," Tommy said. "I don't know if we're jumping to outlandish conclusions about Peter based simply on him getting one piece of legal terminology wrong."

"It would give him a powerful motive to kill Albert Lewis if Albert found out his solicitor, who I presume he was paying handsomely, wasn't even qualified." Evelyn leaned forward. "It would also give the police another suspect to look at instead of Hugh."

"And what about Clara?"

"Tomorrow is Wednesday," Evelyn said. "As David has already pointed out, everyone will be back at work. We cannot leave the house, so we need to instruct someone in London to go to Somerset House for Peter and Clara's marriage certificate. Let's see if we can find out anything about her first husband."

"How will this help Hugh?" David asked.

"Her first husband might not be dead." Tommy walked across the rug. "She might have killed Lewis if she realised that secret could be exposed. Perhaps her husband was a rogue, and she doesn't want a scandal for it to be revealed she was married to him."

"Do people really kill to keep secrets like that quiet?"

Evelyn turned to David. "People have been killed for much less."

"We mustn't forget that Clara Balfour is having a baby. I can imagine there being nothing Peter wouldn't do to keep them both safe."

"Yes." David nodded. "I see that."

"Now, what to do about Hugh?" Tommy faced David. "He has no motive for killing Lewis until he's told the purchase of land was all a wicked ruse. At that point, he has no opportunity to get the cyanide and arrange for Lewis's murder. However, he has a large window of opportunity, as do the rest of us, in the afternoon. Of course, he has no motive at that time."

"What is the cyanide generally kept in?" Evelyn wondered. "A box, or a tin?"

Tommy spread his hands wide. "I really couldn't say."

David shook his head. "Me neither. I must admit, tramping around in a gardener's shed has never interested me."

Evelyn laughed, then grimaced. "No, we are all way too important to know the contents of a garden shed."

"Do you think that is important?"

Evelyn waited until Tommy had got to the end of the rug and turned back to her. "Yes, I do. A person who is aware of how lethal cyanide is wouldn't be likely to grab a handful and carry it back to the house in their fist, would they?"

"Might they wrap it in a handkerchief?" David wondered.

"I don't even know if one can handle the stuff with bare hands or whether gloves should be worn," Tommy said. "How frustrating to be so ill-informed. I shall telephone Partridge first thing in the morning. He can then find out from Joe Noble, our gardener. Hopefully he will let me know pretty quickly."

"Knowledge is always a good thing," Evelyn said. "Once we have that information, I think it will be valuable to think about how the cyanide was brought into the house. Might there still be a quantity still here or has it and the receptacle the killer carried it in been disposed of?"

"Do you have something particular in mind?" Tommy pointed at Evelyn. "You do, I can see it in your face. What do you know?"

"It might mean nothing, but one of the housemaids told Mrs Chapman that there is a vase missing from this room. She reports that it's a particularly repugnant ornament and a putrid green colour, but apparently, it's very valuable. I had thought that someone had taken it because of its value, but now I wonder if it was used to transport the cyanide."

David got to his feet. "I shall let you both get on with your sleuthing. Alex knows many of the same people as me. Perhaps you should ask him to chase up a few of our old chums in London if I'm not back by morning?"

"That's a good idea," Tommy conceded. "I think he's rather keen to do something."

"I should imagine he's enjoying his role as protector but, yes, a task that's a little more active might be good for him."

"It goes without saying that our thoughts, and prayers, go with you, David. We hope to see you back here, with Hugh, soon."

She wished it was possible to make sense of the muddle of things they knew, the pieces of information that seemed to have no connection to anything else and have the answers to their questions immediately. Perhaps then they could identify the actual murderer and they would release Hugh to come home.

~

*G*uilt at Hugh's arrest increased Tommy's desire to find the actual murderer and return Rochester Park to its usual state – better Hugh had a failing estate to save rather than be sitting in a prison cell for a crime Tommy was certain he could not have committed.

"Right," Tommy said, as David left the room to travel to Derby. "Let us go through what we know, what we need to find out, and if there's anything we need other people to do for us."

"We've just spoken about the Balfours. We need someone to visit Somerset House and get a copy of their marriage certificate—we need to know who her first husband was and as much about them and where they are from as we can. If David isn't back, then Alex must ask his London chums if anyone knows more about Peter and his past."

"I know Clara might well be correct and Albert was drunk, but he was so adamant he recognised her. My feeling is there is definitely something there to uncover."

"I agree," Evelyn said. "Now what about the widow?"

"Don't trust her either," Tommy said quickly. "She's not at all upset at his death. She cares more that he didn't leave her all of his money."

"Which brings us to Emma."

"Not so fast," Tommy interjected. "The money would give Louisa an excellent motive to kill Albert and, of course, she had the best opportunity of all to add poison to her husband's medication."

"I can't see her tramping across the snow to the gardener's shed on the off chance she would find poison in there."

"That's a good point," he conceded. "But that would equally hold true for Clara too. She wouldn't consider joining the shoot because of her condition—wouldn't that also preclude her from walking in dangerous conditions?"

"Possibly, but I don't think we can count either of them out simply because they are women." She eyed him with mild reproach. "Now on to Emma."

"I completely agree that any of the women *could* have committed the murder. However, out of the three of them, I think Emma is the most likely. After all, she is the one who inherited the bulk of the estate."

"And she refers to him as 'Albert' all the time. I have never heard her refer to him as 'Mr Lewis'. Not even once. Don't you think that is odd?"

"Extremely." Tommy set off walking back and forth across the rug. "What type of secretary doesn't use her employer's title?"

"One that is very close to him."

"Do we think she was having an affair with him?"

"I can't think of another reason." Evelyn lifted a shoulder. "But if I was to give my impressions after meeting them both, and seeing them together, I would say no. There's something, obviously, but I don't think it's that."

"I also think it's more likely she would bash someone over the head rather than have the patience to sit and pull apart a capsule, add poison, then meticulously fit it back together."

"We've had this conversation before, haven't we? Poison generally seems to be a more likely method of killing for a woman."

Tommy spun on his heel and headed back across the rug. "Yet I don't see Emma committing murder in that way. She seems the sort of woman who would act immediately rather than with great forethought and planning like our murderer."

"Now I haven't had a chance to tell you until now about the other thing Mrs Chapman shared with Cook. It seems Emma does not sleep alone."

Tommy raised an eyebrow. "Well, that's not a surprise in that there always seems to be someone in a bed that isn't theirs in every home we've ever stayed in. Do we know who stays with her?"

"The most likely fellow must be Stanley Cameron. I got the impression during our conversation that he had a crush on Emma. Perhaps his feelings go deeper than that and maybe they are reciprocated."

"Which, I suppose, means we have to consider Stanley and Emma both separately and together as a couple."

"I agree," Evelyn said. "Stanley doesn't have a motive on the face of it, but if he wanted to marry Emma and knew she was going to inherit, then he would have a very big motive. If they worked together, one of them could cover for the other. As Albert's secretary, it would seem likely that Emma knew about his medication."

"And finally, Edwin Granville. Again, hard to imagine him going out into inclement weather to collect poison."

"Yet my talk with Stanley gave me information that shows me that Edwin certainly isn't all he seems."

Tommy raised an eyebrow. "How so?"

"Cameron told me he is certain there is money missing from Albert's business. He says he remembers exactly the deals he was personally involved in and that the monetary value of those deals is not reported accurately by Mr Granville."

"That can't be right. He's such a bumbling old fool. I simply cannot imagine him having the wherewithal to commit such a considered crime as poisoning Lewis."

"Oh, Tommy," Evelyn's voice was so disappointed that he stopped his restless pacing and turned to her enquiringly. "You are not that naïve."

"I know, I know." Tommy grimaced as Evelyn's words reminded him that one should never take a person at face value alone. "We should not blindly accept how people appear to be."

"It's very possible that being forgetful, mislaying his possessions, and acting as though he's losing his marbles is all an act. Believing what we are told without testing the veracity of the information isn't what we do – that's amateur behaviour. We're better than that, Tommy."

"That's what the police have done with Hugh, isn't it? They've taken what is directly in front of them and decided that is fact without testing the strength of their convictions."

Evelyn sighed. "I'm so desperately tired, Tommy. Let's go to bed and see if any of this makes any more sense in the morning."

He walked over to the sofa and put out his hands, then pulled Evelyn to her feet. "We'll get to the heart of this awful business. You know we will. We always do."

"I suppose so."

"Darling, what is it?" Tommy gazed into his wife's face, concern at the apathy in her tone. "You don't sound at all like yourself."

"I shall be fine in the morning." Her voice was stronger, more like her usual confident tone, but Tommy wasn't fooled. "I think I will benefit from a good sleep. I don't feel as though I rested at all last night after Mr Lewis's untimely demise."

"Come along then, let's go up."

"I should check—"

"No," he said firmly. "You should sleep. Whatever it is you think is your duty to check can wait until tomorrow."

He drew her into his arms and pressed a kiss against her temple. Ordinarily she relaxed into his arms, but this evening she remained somewhat aloof. Tommy shook off a feeling of foreboding as he listened to his wife and hoped that uninterrupted sleep would not only help them work out who the murderer was, but that Evelyn would be more herself in the morning.

~

The following morning, after breakfast, Evelyn sat in the drawing room with Elise, Aunt Em, Constance, Grace, and a brooding Alexander Ryder. He appeared as restless as Tommy. Staring out of the window, he whirled around at a quiet knock on the door.

In seconds, he had covered the considerable distance to the door and flung it open.

"Lord Chesden." Malton gave a small, respectful nod, showing no surprise at the force with which Alex gripped the doorknob or the very obvious way he barred entrance to the room by standing with his feet braced shoulder width apart. He tried to peer over Alex's shoulder. "Begging your pardon, but a parcel has been delivered for Miss Constance."

"For me?" Constance asked excitedly. She shot a look at

Alex. "Oh, how very intriguing. Who would send a parcel to me here at Rochester Park?"

Evelyn watched anger take over Alex's face before he breathed deeply through his nose, forced his shoulders to relax, and stepped back from the door so Malton could deliver the package to Constance.

"No word from the police, I suppose, Malton?" Elise asked hopefully.

"I'm afraid not, My Lady," he answered. "The policeman on guard at the front door passed Miss Constance's gift over to me, and I used the opportunity to enquire after Lord Clifford. He was most insistent that he knew nothing."

Evelyn was certain Malton had questioned the uniformed officer thoroughly – he was incredibly loyal to the family and would be as concerned as they were.

On the sofa opposite, Constance tore the plain brown paper from the parcel on her lap and exclaimed with joy at her gift. "Oh, how very charming! I do love chocolates."

She opened the box, glanced up at Alex with an adoring look, then offered the chocolates to Grace. "I couldn't possibly take the first one. Not when the chocolates are so very obviously meant for you."

"Oh, do!" Constance's eyes were bright with happiness. "I'm certain Lord Chesden meant for his very sweet gift to be shared."

Grace chose a sweet and smiled her thanks at her sister. "You're so lucky, Constance."

Constance dropped her eyes demurely. "Thank you, Lord Chesden. It was perfectly lovely of you to arrange for a treat after the terrible few days we've had."

"But I didn't—" Alex moved across the room as swiftly as a tiger stalking its prey. He swiped the box of chocolates from Constance's hands, then grabbed Grace's hand to prevent her from placing the sweet she'd chosen into her mouth.

"Lord Chesden, really!" Elise's voice was high and strained. "What has come over you?"

"I didn't send Miss Christie a gift." He shook his head grimly. "They are not from me."

Grace's hand trembled in his grip. "What does it matter who they are from?"

Evelyn heard the conversation around her but felt as though she was a minute behind them in processing their words. Although she and Tommy had retired relatively early the night before, she did not feel rested. Her head pounded and her eyes were gritty. Exhaustion meant her brain was not working as quickly as usual.

"I didn't send them," he repeated. "Who else would send your sister chocolates. Who else knows she's here?"

"Malton," Aunt Em said with authority. "Please take the chocolates and the paper they were wrapped in and put them on the table. Then fetch Lord Northmoor immediately."

"Yes, My Lady." Malton hurried over and stooped to collect the few sweets that had fallen from the box. He replaced them and took the brown paper from the sofa next to Constance.

"Where, precisely, did that package come from?" Alex asked. Fury stained his words.

"The uniformed officer brought it into the hall while you were at breakfast, My Lord. As soon as I was aware you were settled in here, I retrieved the package and brought it straight to Miss Constance."

"Where did he get it from?" Alex barked.

"I don't know the answer to that, I'm afraid." For the first time since Evelyn had met him, the butler looked rattled, his usual calm demeanour transformed into an air of worry.

"We need that officer in here," Alex said urgently. "Lord Northmoor will want to question him. Where is he?"

Evelyn blinked as Alex addressed her, and her befuddled

brain finally made sense of what was happening. *What was wrong with her?* "He went to use the telephone."

"I will find him." Malton put the box of chocolates and the paper they had been wrapped in on the table and hurried from the room.

"Evelyn?" Aunt Em leaned towards her and put a hand on her knee. "What is it? Are you unwell?"

"I'm tired," she said automatically, giving no thought to how she felt.

Aunt Em nodded but did not look convinced. "You believe someone has poisoned the chocolates meant for Constance, Lord Chesden?"

"That is my concern," he answered. He had now taken hold of himself, his earlier white-hot anger under control.

"Who would do such a thing?" Constance cried.

"Someone who wants to stop you – permanently – from remembering what you saw on Christmas night when you were outside with Lord Chesden." Evelyn got to her feet and pulled the rope on the right-hand side of the fireplace. "I need strong coffee. Now is not the time for me to be so tired I can't concentrate on solving this crime."

"But I saw nothing," Constance said. "At least I don't think that I did."

"I don't suppose the murderer can take that risk," Alex said quietly.

"Lord Northmoor will be exceedingly grateful for your quick thinking," Evelyn told Alex. "I am only sorry I am so weary the thought did not occur to me first."

"My Lady?" A maid bobbed her knee at the doorway, her eyes on Elise.

"Coffee," Elise instructed. "Hot, strong, and plenty of it, please."

The girl hurried off, and moments later, Tommy rushed into the room. "Is everyone alright?"

"I'm afraid I was of absolutely no use," Evelyn said. "Lord

Chesden acted very quickly and prevented Grace from eating the chocolate she chose."

"The box of sweets and the paper they were wrapped in are on the table," Malton said as he came into the room behind Tommy.

Tommy hurried over. "Evelyn, have you looked at the paper?"

She walked over to join him and looked down at the plain brown paper spread out on the table. Constance's name was printed in block letters, followed by a line that proclaimed: c/o Rochester Park.

Elise jumped to her feet and rushed over to a very handsome Victorian walnut writing desk. She pulled up the domed front. "There's a box missing!" She covered her face with trembling hands. "The police will blame me. Oh, who is doing this to us?"

"Elise?" Evelyn asked as she walked over to put a comforting arm around the girl's shoulders. "What do you mean?"

"I bought a box of chocolates for every lady who was staying with us." She pointed a tremulous finger at the boxes stacked neatly inside the writing desk. "I intended to write a little note with each gift. There should be three: one each for Mrs Lewis, Mrs Balfour and Miss Mountjoy, but there's only two here."

Evelyn understood Elise's fear. The police had arrested Hugh based on their belief that he had a solid motive for wanting Albert Lewis dead, and now the only potential witness to the shadowy figure outside the house before dinner had been sent chocolates that Elise kept in her writing desk.

Who else would have known they were there? And more to the point, who would've had access to them and sent them to Constance?

CHAPTER 9

Terror gripped Tommy's stomach as he looked around the room at his family to assure himself no one was injured. Elise and Grace looked close to tears, Alex appeared to be barely holding on to his temper, Constance was stunned, Aunt Em grim, but Evelyn's demeanour shocked him most. She looked completely devastated. Her blue eyes were wide with horror. The dark bruises underneath were proof she had slept much less than he had.

He reached out and took hold of her hand. "Do you need to lie down? Perhaps Doris could go with you. I would be quite content to trust Doris and Nancy to keep you safe."

Evelyn looked uncomfortably around the room, even though he had spoken too quietly for anyone else to hear. "I'm sure coffee will revive me."

He nodded, though he was not convinced. Years of marriage told him arguing with Evelyn would not change her mind, but simply make her more stubborn. She was as determined as ever to find the murderer, despite clearly not feeling her best.

"Do you have brown paper like this in the house?"

"Yes." Elise rummaged in the desk. "I bought some to wrap the three boxes, but it is missing."

"You're certain there were only three boxes?"

"Of course," Elise answered. "I bought Christmas presents for the family separately. I wanted to buy our guests a little something but as I didn't know any of them before they arrived, it seemed something generic like chocolates would be the best choice of gift."

"I'm sorry to keep checking up on you, but you're absolutely positive the paper was in the desk too. You wouldn't have kept it somewhere else?"

"I'm sure." She lifted a silver fountain pen. "This isn't mine, though. I can't think how it has got in here."

Tommy walked over to Elise. "May I look at it?"

"It looks like it fits the description of the pen Edwin Granville told me yesterday he had lost."

"That old fool would lose his own head if it wasn't attached," Aunt Em scoffed.

"You're quite correct," Evelyn said. "Though it seems rather odd that it would turn up here in Elise's desk."

Evelyn had not said that Edwin's cufflink was found next to Albert's body – it was probably best they kept that information to themselves. As far as he was aware, the police hadn't yet discovered it. His conscience poked at him. With this additional evidence, he should really tell the police, though would they now think the cufflink and the pen had been somewhat clumsily planted by the family in order to throw suspicion on Edwin and off Hugh?

"Why would Edwin want to kill Constance?" Alex asked. His voice was low, but it was clear he was barely containing his anger. "Unless he was the one who left the footprints in the snow as he fetched the cyanide to kill Albert Lewis."

Tommy held up a hand. "I don't think we should speculate or jump to conclusions at this stage."

"Things are rarely as they seem," Evelyn added. "Until we

have gathered all the information we need to solve a murder, things always seem to point in the direction the murderer wants us to look."

A knock sounded on the door, and everyone's head turned to look in that direction. It was opened by Malton, who admitted a maid with a heavily laden tray and Detective Sergeant Bishop.

"I've spoken to our man outside," the detective said with no preamble. "It seems that the chocolates were on the steps when he went outside this morning."

Tommy frowned. "He wasn't out there all night?"

"He was stationed at the door," the detective said defensively. "More correctly, I should state that his colleague, Barnes, spent the night standing on the inside guarding the door. At change of shift, Harris went outside, and Barnes went to rest."

"So, what you're saying is that the chocolates could have been left outside at any time between Barnes going on shift last night and Harris's beginning this morning?"

"That is correct." Bishop nodded. "Though there is now a police officer guarding the back door after we realised people could exit the house that way."

Elise pointed to the double doors leading out onto the patio. "Were those doors secured?"

Detective Sergeant Bishop looked confused. "They weren't guarded specifically, Lady Clifford. But Barnes, standing immediately inside the front door, would have seen someone entering the drawing room."

"Perhaps you need to get the fellow up and question him thoroughly," Tommy advised. "Was he really there all night or is it possible he might have had to answer a call of nature or some other errand?"

"I'm sure Barnes fulfilled his duties impeccably." Bishop's expression showed that he wasn't nearly as certain as his words.

As soon as he left the room carrying the chocolates and the brown paper, Elise moved over to the tray to pour coffee. "Shouldn't you have told him about the pen, Tommy?"

"I should have, yes." Tommy looked at his cousin in consternation. "But I think leaving Granville's pen in your desk is a rather clumsy attempt to frame him."

"How can you know that?" Alex asked.

"It isn't the first time his possessions have been found in a compromising place," Tommy explained. "I am afraid I can't say any more than that."

"Does that mean he isn't the murderer?" Elise gave Evelyn a cup of coffee and then walked over to the desk and closed it with a resounding bang.

"Someone could be trying to frame him as Tommy said," Evelyn said. "But we can't rule out the possibility he's doing it on purpose, so it appears that someone is trying to make him look guilty."

"Is he clever enough to do that?" Aunt Em asked. "It seems to me that he's quite dotty."

"I rather think the 'silly old buffoon' persona is a character he plays." Tommy raised an eyebrow. "I think he's a shrewd old chap who we shouldn't write off."

"Is there anyone you *can* write off?" Alex said, frustration making his words harsh.

"Family, obviously." Tommy smiled. "But there are six main suspects, none of which we can discount at this time. I've made some telephone calls and hopefully we'll receive some answers later in the day."

"Good." Constance shuddered. "I should like to go home."

"We are doing our best," Tommy said grimly. "I would like us all to get home too, Constance. The sooner the better."

Elise glanced at Evelyn. "You too, Ev?"

"No," Evelyn shook her head. "I said I would stay and

help you, Elise. I will not leave until I've fulfilled my promise."

Tommy wanted to pack his entire family up that very moment and take them all back to Yorkshire, away from this house and the murderer whose actions were keeping them imprisoned.

The last thing he wanted was for his dear wife to remain at Rochester Park even after they had uncovered the killer – which he was certain they would. She looked so pale and frail. He knew, however, that if he insisted she come back to Hessleham Hall with the rest of the family, she would dig her heels in and refuse.

He could only hope that when the killer was caught, Evelyn would regain her usual vitality and whatever it was that had her looking so ill would pass quickly.

~

"Mrs O'Connell," Evelyn said sharply. "It is nearly eleven. We agreed you were to rest this morning!"

The cook looked up from the stove with a guilty expression. "You're early, Lady Northmoor. Good morning, Miss Constance."

Evelyn waved a hand at the wooden table and looked at her sister-in-law. "Sit down, my dear. I shall make a refreshing pot of tea for us all."

"Was the coffee not to your liking, Lady Northmoor?" Mrs O'Connell asked, a worried expression on her lined face. "Lady Clifford sent for it not half an hour ago."

"I wanted coffee." Evelyn grimaced. "In fact, it was me who asked for it. But when it came, the smell of it made me quite queasy."

"Really?" The cook cocked an eyebrow at Evelyn. "I wonder why that might be."

"I'm afraid I'm not feeling quite myself," Evelyn admitted.

"You do look a bit peaky, My Lady."

Constance watched the discussion avidly before moving over to stand next to Cook. "Why don't you both sit down and rest? *I* will make the tea."

Evelyn flapped a hand in front of her face. "It's rather hot in here, don't you think? I think I will take a seat."

Constance lifted a shoulder. "It's a kitchen, Ev. It's always extremely warm in a kitchen."

"Have you eaten?" Mrs O'Connell peered at her.

"No." Evelyn pulled a face. "I couldn't stomach anything. Isn't it strange how being horribly tired makes you feel so bilious you can't eat even though you're positively starving?"

The cook patted an ample hip before she sat opposite Evelyn. "I've never had that problem, My Lady. I've sometimes been so weary I couldn't manage to walk upstairs to bed, but tiredness has never affected me so badly that I've lost my appetite."

Constance busied herself putting the huge kettle onto the hob to boil and preparing a small tray with a teapot, jug of milk, sugar bowl, and cups and saucers. "If you're hungry, you should really try to eat something, Ev. Maybe something plain to settle your stomach?"

"I can easily make you a slice of toast if you think it would help, Lady Northmoor?" Cook put her hands on the table to help lever herself back upright.

Evelyn pointed at her. "You're not to get up! Perhaps I might try a dry biscuit, if you have one? Miss Constance will fetch it for me."

Mrs O'Connell's brow furrowed in concentration. "There's none of the shortbread left I made yesterday. The police have quite voracious appetites, let me tell you."

"Everyone has a ferocious appetite for your shortbread." Constance laughed. "Lord Chesden has commented on more than one occasion he will be extremely sad to return home to London and leave behind your cooking."

Cook smiled. "What a charming young man. I'm flattered."

"He *is* rather charming."

Evelyn smiled at the look of adoration on Constance's face. Not for the first time, she hoped and prayed that Alexander Ryder had truly shed the more unpleasant aspects of his personality and was a man worthy of Constance's affections.

"He acted very quickly today," Evelyn said. "Goodness only knows what would have happened if he hadn't."

"Oh, my goodness." Mrs O'Connell put a hand on her chest. "What happened?"

"We think someone poisoned a box of chocolates meant for Miss Constance."

"We don't really know that, though, do we?" Constance asked bravely. "Alex may have overreacted."

"*Lord Chesden*," Evelyn deliberately emphasised Alex's title, "acted extremely intelligently." Tommy wouldn't be happy to hear his sister use Alex's Christian name in front of the family, but he'd be furious if he knew she had slipped up in front of staff. "There is no reason for anyone to deliver chocolates to you here. They were not sent in the post but left on the doorstep. It is common sense to believe they have been contaminated."

"I don't know why whoever it is would want to scare us all like that." Constance's face, already flushed with embarrassment, grew pinker with her words. "It's not as if I saw a thing!"

"Perhaps the murderer can't be sure you didn't. Maybe they thought you *had* seen them. Don't forget you were standing near the house, so would have been in the light, whereas they were in the dark. Sometimes it's not what you've seen that's helpful, but what you've heard, or even a smell. It's not unusual for a memory to come back when hearing that sound or experiencing a similar scent."

"I wish I had seen them," Constance said fervently. "Then I could just tell the police and it would all be over. I'm rather scared to think someone might have tried to kill me. I thought Tommy and Aunt Em were overreacting by asking Lord Chesden to look after me."

"I'm certain it must be terrifying," Mrs O'Connell murmured. "What a wicked person it must be to cause a young lady to be so frightened."

Constance took the teapot over to the stove and rested it on a chopping board while she poured water over the tea leaves. Carrying it back to the table, she stirred the pot before replacing the lid. "Shall I pour?"

"Best to let it stew for a few minutes, Miss Constance." Cook advised. "Perhaps you could look in the pantry and see if there are any biscuits for Lady Northmoor?"

"Yes, of course." Constance hurried over in the direction Cook indicated. She returned with two very plain biscuits on a saucer. "This is all I could find."

"Perfect." Mrs O'Connell nodded in satisfaction. "I made these for one of the housemaids. Poor thing came from the workhouse into service, and I don't think the child has ever developed a taste for sugar. She prefers everything she eats to be plain."

"How dreadful," Constance said. "Hasn't she tried your shortbread? If it can keep a grown man from London, it can surely tempt her?"

They all laughed, and Evelyn gratefully nibbled a biscuit. "Thank you. This is perfect. As much as I adore Mrs O'Connell's baking, I don't think I could stomach anything with sugar or too much flavour today."

"I'll pour your tea first," Constance said hurriedly. "Weak tea will surely settle your stomach."

Mrs O'Connell peered at Evelyn. "You do look like you

have a little colour now, Lady Northmoor. Perhaps, if I could be so bold, you would benefit from a lie-down this afternoon?"

"I probably would," Evelyn agreed. "In fact, Lord Northmoor suggested I go upstairs with Doris and Nancy as companions. As lovely as that sounds, I'd much rather put my time in uncovering the murderer so Lord Clifford can come home and poor Lady Clifford can relax. What a dreadful thing to happen the first time she entertains!"

"Do you have a plan?" Constance asked.

"Yes." Evelyn took a small sip of tea. "We need to speak to everyone again and wait for the answers to some questions Lord Northmoor asked this morning."

"Are we allowed to know what he asked?"

"We have asked some friends in London to go to Somerset House and find out the name of Mrs Balfour's first husband. It might not be important, but it could have significance. The only way to find out is for us to learn who he was. The marriage certificate will hopefully also give us a clue as to what area of London she lived in."

Constance nodded. "That's important because it might give you a clue how Mr Lewis knew her?"

"We hope so. Though, of course, that might be a dead end. Perhaps Mr Lewis didn't know Mrs Balfour at all. It's possible she simply looks like someone else."

"I think the way you and Tommy find murderers is fascinating."

"It may well be," Evelyn said, pinning Constance with a serious gaze. "But it can also be dangerous. Please don't go poking around for information, especially after what happened this morning."

"No fear!" Constance shook her head emphatically. "I intend to do exactly as my brother instructed and stay close to Lord Chesden. While I admire what you and Tommy do, I'd like to stay alive long enough to receive a proposal from a handsome fellow and have a fabulous wedding."

Evelyn wished she had nothing else on her mind but the same type of fun things as Constance. However, she couldn't help but worry if she herself had eaten something meant to cause her harm.

Although she hadn't dropped down dead like Albert Lewis after taking his blood pressure tablets, she felt quite dreadful. It wasn't like her to be unwell. She normally had such a hearty constitution. Neither was it very convenient to be ill when Tommy needed her to help investigate.

~

Tommy stalked into the library, where he found Peter Balfour and Edwin Granville sitting together. "Would you mind awfully excusing us, Mr Granville? Coffee is being served in the drawing room."

Peter Balfour got to his feet. "I should like coffee."

"Please sit down, Mr Balfour. What I have to say won't take long. I venture there will still be coffee left when we are finished."

Peter sat and shot a helpless look at Edwin's retreating back. "So much for sticking together."

Tommy barked out a laugh. "He said that?"

Peter smiled despite himself. "Yes, he said we should stay together so the murderer couldn't target us."

"Where is your wife?" It wasn't the question Tommy intended to ask first, but as it occurred to him he didn't want his own family alone in the house, it seemed strange Balfour didn't have the same concern for his own wife.

"She has stayed in bed this morning." Balfour looked down at the floor. "You know, women's issues, with the baby and whatever."

"Is she quite safe?"

"Certainly." Peter's gaze snapped up to meet Tommy's. "I'm not an idiot, man! I locked her in the bedroom so she would stay out of harm's way."

Tommy could just imagine Evelyn's reaction if he suggested she stayed locked in their room for safekeeping! "I see. Well, that is between you and your wife. If you are both happy with that arrangement, it is certainly none of my business."

"What was it you wanted to discuss, Lord Northmoor? I really should check on my wife."

Strange. Moments earlier, the man was happy to stay with Edwin Granville with no thoughts of his wife locked away upstairs!

"May I ask what you did after arriving at Rochester Park on Christmas Day?"

"We unpacked, then while Clara had a nap, I came downstairs to speak to Mr Lewis. I was with him the entire time before I went back up to dress for dinner. I presume you wish to know this so you can see who does and does not have an alibi for the time the poison was taken from the gardener's shed?"

"That is correct."

"As you can tell, my time is accounted for," Peter said stiffly.

It was no less than Tommy expected. The man had certainly had enough time to create an alibi for himself. Though Peter Balfour's rather depended on a man who couldn't verify it one way or another.

"Where did you train to become a solicitor?"

Peter blinked at the sudden change of direction in Tommy's questions. "Wh—what has that to do with anything?"

"Can you answer the question?"

"Of course I can answer it," Peter blustered. "I simply don't know why you're asking."

"I don't think you're a qualified solicitor," Tommy said easily.

Peter crossed his arms across his chest. "How dare you! What gives you the right to make such a scurrilous accusation?"

"My cousin-in-law was a solicitor in London until recently. He had never heard of you before he arrived here."

"Oh, oh I see." Peter nodded his head violently. "If all the lords in London haven't heard of me, then I must be a fraud."

"None of David's friends who practice as solicitors are lords," Tommy said. "However, they have all worked at various firms for years and your name is not known to them."

"How do you think I got a job with Albert Lewis if I wasn't qualified?" Peter stared at Tommy with a supercilious expression. "He wouldn't have employed me without the correct credentials."

"I should think a man as clever as yourself could easily have concocted references."

"I'm sure I could have," Peter agreed. "But I didn't."

"Who was your wife's first husband?"

If Peter was shocked at the first change in Tommy's line of questioning, this one made him furious. His nostrils flared and his foot tapped an angry tattoo on the floor. "That is none of your business."

"Do you know his name?" Tommy asked, not caring if he was goading the other man.

"Of course, I do!"

"And did he die or was there an embarrassing divorce?"

"I believe your wife has already asked that question. Clara was a widow when we married."

It wasn't difficult for Tommy to arrange his features into sombre lines. "I suppose he died in the war."

"Actually, he did not," Peter retorted.

"A tragic accident then, perhaps?" Tommy pressed.

"Yes," Peter spat out angrily. "That is exactly what it was.

Now, if you will excuse me, Lord Northmoor, I must check on my wife."

As soon as he received word from London about the name of Clara Balfour's first husband, he must find out how to search for news articles about the man's death. Surely someone in his acquaintance would know how to do that.

If he trusted what Peter told him, the lawyer had an alibi that could only be verified by a man that was now dead and his wife had none.

CHAPTER 10

The tea and biscuit had settled Evelyn's stomach. Although she didn't feel her usual self, she was much recovered.

When she came back upstairs, she found Emma Mountjoy alone in the library with a book in her hand.

"Good morning, Miss Mountjoy. How are you this morning?"

Emma looked at her, then gave that enigmatic smile of hers. "I should say I am better than you, Lady Northmoor. Haven't you slept?"

Evelyn pulled a face. "I confess I find it difficult to sleep when there is a murderer on the loose. Don't you?"

"Not at all," Emma said easily.

"Is that because you have someone close at hand to protect you?"

To Evelyn's surprise, Emma's response to her rather impertinent question was to burst into laughter. "My goodness, Lady Northmoor, how very perceptive of you."

Evelyn didn't think it was necessary to explain how she knew about Emma's nocturnal habits. They were, of course, none of her business. Although she needed to ask in case it was relevant to the investigation.

"Ordinarily I feel quite safe in my own bedroom, but I suppose poor Mr Lewis thought he was somewhat protected in his too."

"The reason I don't feel in any danger, Lady Northmoor, is because I am not a target. It stands to reason that the only person who could have killed Albert for his money is me, because I am the one who inherited. I know I didn't kill him. And, even if I did, I am hardly likely to kill myself."

"You believe Mr Lewis was killed for another reason?"

"Yes, though I don't know what the motive was."

"I suppose you have considered the possibility that the person you are involved with could be the perpetrator. Perhaps he killed Mr Lewis to get his hands on Lewis's money through you?"

Emma smiled. "I see what you are doing, Lady Northmoor. You are attempting to trip me into admitting I have a beau, and the name of that person."

"I am trying to do no such thing," Evelyn replied. "You and I both know the person sharing your bedroom is Mr Stanley Cameron."

Emma's face lost some of its confidence before she visibly rallied. "What of it?"

"Do you trust Mr Cameron so very much?"

"Yes," Emma said vehemently. "He is completely devoted to me."

"Yet when you marry, he will have access to an exceedingly large sum of money. Doesn't that make you feel a little uncomfortable?"

"Stanley loved me before I became an heiress," Emma said, but her tone had lost some of its confidence. "He will continue to love me now."

"I am sure that is true." Evelyn reached out a hand to rest on Emma's arm. "But it would be prudent to protect yourself, wouldn't it? I would advise you to take legal advice and make a will immediately."

"It's a little late for that," Emma whispered. "Stanley and I are already married."

"Oh my dear," Evelyn said. "Why did you keep it a secret?"

"Albert wanted me to have all the advantages that money brings – things he could never have hoped to have at my age. You must know better than anyone else, Lady Northmoor. Money really does bring you everything you want."

She was living proof that it most certainly did not. If it did, then she and Tommy would have had a child by now. "I'm afraid I still don't understand why you didn't tell Mr Lewis about your marriage."

"He didn't have money when he was a young man. When he had money, he realised that wasn't all he wanted. He wanted a place in society and to be respected."

"He married Louisa thinking he would get that?"

"Yes, he thought marriage to a woman from a good family would guarantee him that. Louisa married him because he was filthy rich and for no other reason. It certainly wasn't because she wanted to give him an heir."

Emma certainly seemed to know a lot about her employer and his personal life. There was more to their relationship than simply business. Could a personal relationship between Albert and Emma be why she kept her marriage secret from him? Evelyn turned the facts around in her head – they still didn't fit. Men like Albert Lewis simply didn't leave their entire estate to their mistress, did they?

"You're his daughter, aren't you?"

Emma gasped and stared at Evelyn in dismay. "How did you know?"

"You have consistently referred to him as Albert rather than Mr Lewis, which is rather odd behaviour for a secretary. In addition, what you have just said about him wanting more for you – things only money can buy – is the sort of thing a father wants for his child."

"Albert didn't want anyone to know." Emma pulled a handkerchief from a small bag on the floor next to her chair and dabbed at her eyes. "He and my mother were never married. She had hoped they would be when his first wife died, but Albert was so busy chasing his dreams of being accepted in society he married Louisa. Mother was quite devastated."

"I'm sure that must have been desperately hard for her," Evelyn said. "And for you too, of course."

"He sent her an allowance for my care." Emma's mouth twisted. "It wasn't what I wanted because it was no substitute for a father. But it allowed me to get an education."

"And he then employed you when you had completed your education?"

"He knew he could trust me, you see. Not only was I family, but it was ultimately in my interests to be loyal and hard-working because one day the company would be mine."

"Did you always know that?"

"Oh yes. Albert was very open about that. On my very first day working for him, he told me I was his principal beneficiary. So, you see, if I was going to kill Albert, I could have done it at any time since then."

Evelyn bit her lip in consternation. "Have you told the police this information?"

"I have not." Emma blew her nose. "Can you imagine what they would make of it? They would assume that I, an illegitimate girl with nothing to my name, had killed my father to inherit his fortune."

Or, if they knew it all, they might think that she had been taken advantage of by Stanley Cameron so he could access Lewis's money through marriage to Emma. Had Stanley killed Albert, and if so, did that mean that Emma was next?

"I agree the police would look more closely at you, and

indeed Mr Cameron, if they knew the full truth," Evelyn said carefully. "Are you aware of Mr Cameron's belief that your father's accountant is embezzling funds?"

Anger blazed in Emma's eyes. "I am. As soon as everything is finalised, I will terminate his employment."

"Is that wise?" Evelyn continued quickly before Emma could interrupt. "Obviously you do not want someone working for you who is stealing, but perhaps it is more sensible for you to catch him in the act."

"He's an old man. I'm not sure I want the police involved." Emma looked doubtfully at Evelyn. "I thought perhaps I could rid myself of his services with as little fuss as possible."

"Have you considered if your father was aware Mr Granville was taking money from him? That puts a rather different slant on the events over the last few days. It's certainly a motive for murder, isn't it?"

"I suppose I rather ruled him out as a suspect because of his age and his demeanour."

"Lord Northmoor and I wondered the same thing," Evelyn admitted. "Though if you and Mr Cameron are correct and he has a scheme for stealing money, he's not quite as scatter-brained as he makes himself out to be, is he?"

"No." Emma shivered. "I see that now."

"I implore you to be careful, Miss Mountjoy." Evelyn wanted to say so much more. "Being wealthy makes you extremely vulnerable to unscrupulous people who will want to take advantage of your new circumstances."

"I trust Stanley," Emma said firmly. "But I thank you for your concern."

Evelyn got to her feet. "Thank you for speaking to me."

Emma did not reply, concern etched on her face. Evelyn left the library not knowing whether she had just talked to a murderess, someone in cahoots with her secret husband, or an extremely frightened young woman.

Tommy had about run out of ways to speak to Mrs Lewis when he was handed the opportunity by a very unlikely source. The widow had been ensconced in her room all day but left to speak to Detective Sergeant Bishop.

He took her into the drawing room as soon as she exited the room the detectives were using for their questioning. "I thought you would like a drink after your ordeal. Perhaps a sherry?"

She gazed at him with distrust. "Actually, Lord Northmoor, I would like a large brandy."

Malton, standing in the hallway, looked at Tommy enquiringly. "It's alright, Malton, I shall get the drinks for Mrs Lewis and myself."

"Goodness," she said in a scathing voice. "I didn't know men of your standing poured their own drinks."

"Of course we do," Tommy said easily. "We can even wash and dress ourselves too."

She pressed her lips together tightly. Tommy didn't know whether it was because he had mentioned personal ablutions or because he hadn't risen to her barb. He rather thought a tendency towards piousness was simply her personality.

"Make it a large one."

Tommy poured Mrs Lewis a double brandy and a small measure for himself. After all, it wasn't yet lunchtime. "I'm very sorry for your inconvenience. I'm sure you would like to be at home mourning your husband in private."

She looked surprised at his perceptiveness. "Yes. I would actually. Instead of being kept here like some sort of prisoner. I imagine this place to be like the Tower of London – uncomfortable, cold, and full of criminals and other lowlifes."

"I hope you don't count me amongst the latter." He waited for Mrs Lewis to take a seat and then sat opposite.

"Who knows?" She shrugged. "Someone killed my husband, why not you?"

"I have absolutely no motive," Tommy said evenly, determined not to allow the woman's rudeness to make him cross. "If it interests you, I do have an alibi both for the time before dinner on Christmas Day and for last night when chocolates were left outside for my sister."

"The policeman told me about that." She took a sip of brandy, showing no effects whatsoever as she swallowed, and the liquid made its way down her throat. "Nasty business if the sweets were poisoned. I saw how dreadfully Albert suffered."

"Do you have an alibi for either occasion?"

"Absolutely not," she answered, with no trace of either guilt or concern. "Albert came straight downstairs to talk business when we arrived, leaving me completely alone. I *didn't* take a trip outside in the snow to fetch poison though before you ask."

"No." Tommy crossed his legs at the ankles. "I suspect you are the type of woman who would've waited until the Boxing Day shoot and used a gun to kill your husband."

"Precisely." She laughed then and, although it was extremely inappropriate, it transformed her face from permanently disapproving to attractive and for the first time since he'd met her, Tommy could see what had drawn Albert Lewis to his wife. Other than her family connections, of course. "Easy enough for a woman to have an issue with her gun and it be staged as a perfectly ghastly accident."

"What about last night and this morning?" he asked. "Where were you in the time frame when the chocolates were delivered?"

"I expect I was in bed." She lifted a shoulder in resignation. "By myself, unlike everyone else in this house, I should imagine. But I didn't do it. I didn't poison Albert, so I had no need to kill your sister. If I was going to kill anyone, it would be that silly child who has all of Albert's money."

"What are your thoughts about your husband's staff?"

"Granville is a fool, but I expect you already know that. He's a quite stupid man. Balfour would do anything for Albert, but I don't trust his wife. There's something very chilling about that one. As for Cameron, I warned Albert over and over not to trust him. He's calculating and has an eye on moving himself up in the world by any means necessary."

"Who do you think did it?" he asked nonchalantly.

"If I enjoyed a wager, my money would be on Stanley Cameron. He's ambitious. Perhaps he has designs on that unattractive girl who now has all of my Albert's money."

"What will you do now?"

"I have a home and a generous allowance. As far as I am aware, that doesn't change whether I stay single or remarry." She twisted in her seat and looked out of the window. "I think I should like a proper husband, even though it's too late for me to have children now. Albert didn't want them. Isn't that odd?"

"Yes," Tommy said gently, slightly embarrassed at Louisa's show of emotion. It was obvious she had turned away from him because she was weeping. "It's very unusual."

Her behaviour since her husband's death had been very hard to understand, but he thought he knew now why she had acted the way she had. She must have been aware Albert had married her to increase his social standing. Although she had denied in their earlier conversation that they moved to Derbyshire because Albert was having an affair in London, the rumours must have been difficult for her to bear. She had married a man who had no intention of treating her properly. It was no wonder she was bitter.

"There we have it, Lord Northmoor. The upshot is I don't have an alibi for either of the timescales. I clearly have a motive for Albert's death. He wasn't a good husband, and I wasn't aware until yesterday that I wasn't his sole beneficiary." She turned her tear-streaked face back to his. "But I would never do something to hurt your sister. She appears to be a very sweet, if somewhat naïve, young lady. I hope you can believe that."

He blinked at the double-edged compliment towards Constance. "I hope you can believe that I am truly sorry about your losses, Mrs Lewis."

She gave a sharp nod, finished her brandy, and left the room.

Although he pitied her, Tommy couldn't cross her off their suspect list. Her motive for killing her husband had only increased in his eyes during their conversation.

~

*E*velyn had almost given up trying to find Stanley Cameron after a fruitless search through the downstairs rooms of Rochester Park. It was Malton who gave her the man's location. She should have asked him first – the butler didn't miss a thing.

She waited outside the room downstairs that had been used by the former butler before he had resigned following the death of Hugh's father. The butler's room contained the telephone and apparently Cameron had told Malton he had several important business calls to make.

The door opened, and Evelyn got to her feet, smiling a greeting. "I wondered who was in there."

"I am sorry, Lady Northmoor," he said deferentially. "Have you been waiting to use the telephone?"

"One of the housemaids brought me something to sit on." She indicated the chair behind her. "I have been quite comfortable."

"Even so, I have monopolised the telephone this morning. For that I do apologise."

Evelyn didn't correct his assumption she had been waiting for some time. "To be honest, I should probably have written notes rather than make calls. My husband always tells me how much people appreciate a nice handwritten letter."

"I'm sure that's correct." He smiled. "Though for a businessman, using the telephone is much quicker and easier."

"I'm sure." Evelyn recalled a clause in Albert Lewis's will. "I understand you are to run Mr Lewis's company for the next year. What a very great responsibility for you."

"He taught me well," Stanley said. "I am looking forward to the challenge."

"I'm certain you and your wife will be very busy over the next year."

His eyes narrowed. "Have you been snooping?"

"I don't snoop," she said haughtily. "Your wife told me herself."

He shook his head in denial. "I can't believe Emma would do that."

"She appears thrilled with the arrangement." Evelyn assessed the young man. "You, however, don't seem quite so enthused."

He pulled a hand through his hair. "It's dangerous, don't you see? If the police find out, they will think one or both of us arranged for Albert's death."

"Has Detective Sergeant Bishop spoken to you yet about the chocolates left on the front step of the house this morning?"

His brow furrowed in confusion. "I don't know what you mean. What chocolates?"

"Left for my sister-in-law," Evelyn said. "Most likely poisoned to stop her from identifying whoever it was tramping over the lawn to the gardener's shed."

"I'm sorry to hear that," he said. "But I know nothing about it."

"What alibi will you tell the police?"

He shook his head in consternation. "I don't know what you mean, Lady Northmoor."

"I presume the reason you didn't leave the chocolates on the doorstep is because you were with your wife all night and so didn't have an opportunity to sneak out of the house to leave them there. However, you can hardly tell the police that, can you?"

Understanding dawned behind his dark eyes. "I don't know what I can tell them."

"What about the afternoon you arrived at Rochester Hall? Do you have an alibi for that time?"

"I was downstairs talking to Mr Lewis for most of the afternoon."

Evelyn lifted an eyebrow. "Oddly, Mr Balfour has used the exact same alibi. Were the three of you speaking together?"

"Absolutely not," he retorted adamantly. "Mr Lewis had no need to discuss anything with Balfour. He had no intention of completing the deal for Lord Clifford's land, so why would he need his solicitor?"

"That's an extremely good question." She smiled to soften her next words. "However, you must see that your alibi is a dead man. That's not very helpful to a man in your position, is it?"

He pulled a hand through his hair again, leaving even more strands sticking up. "I have no alibi for the murder of a man whose death leaves my wife an heiress. My *secret* wife. If we tell the police now we are married, we'll look even more guilty. As though we have something to hide and the person we were hiding our relationship from is now dead. What a mess."

"It is rather," Evelyn agreed. "What do you intend to do about it?"

"I don't know," he said honestly.

Evelyn pointed at the open door to the butler's room. "You have made no telephone calls that help you?"

"I told you," he said harshly. "I have been making business calls."

"I shouldn't imagine the police will remain as clueless as they currently are for long," she said. "Anyone with two eyes in their head can see exactly how you and Miss Mountjoy feel about each other."

He wanted to correct her given she was the only person in on their secret and insist that Emma be given her proper title, but he stopped short. "They seem pretty incompetent to me. Lord Clifford is about as least likely a murderer as they can hope to find."

"You're quite correct," Evelyn agreed. "Lord Clifford doesn't have it in him to kill another person. He's an exceedingly gentle man. He is not, however, an idiot."

"Is that your way of warning me?"

"Please don't try to pull off the sort of deal Albert Lewis put to him unless you mean to follow through."

"You know why he did that. He thought being at a holiday retreat with three earls would help people see him as a gentleman. Albert Lewis did not understand that you can't buy your way into the upper echelons of society."

"That isn't the sort of deal you want to make in your new position as manager?"

"No." He shook his head decisively. "And as I've said, it wasn't an 'Albert Lewis' type of deal, either. Your friend will have to find some other way to save his estate."

"Do you have any ideas?"

He raised his eyebrows. "Are you asking my advice as a businessman, Lady Northmoor? Don't you people have men you pay lots of money for giving you guidance?"

She ignored the jibe. "I do not know the details of every single person my husband pays money to. I certainly don't know Lord Clifford's personal arrangements. The reason I asked you the question is that Miss Mountjoy told me you had worked for Mr Lewis for years. Perhaps it will take the knowledge of a man outside our social circle to think of a way to help Lord Clifford. After all, we could not think of a way to help."

"He needs to use the estate to make money for him. He has lots of land simply sitting there doing nothing. I assume you have thought about hosting shoots and charging? Lots of people would pay to come somewhere like this."

"That was Tommy's idea for the Boxing Day shoot. We were hopeful Mr Lewis would tell his business acquaintances about the good time he had here." She pulled a wry face. "Now there's been a murder no one will want to come anywhere near Rochester Park."

"You may find the opposite is true," Stanley said. "Some people can be rather ghoulish and would like to visit Rochester Park simply to see the room in which Mr Lewis died. My advice, for what it is worth, would be to advertise traditional English shoots in the American newspapers. They are fascinated by all things English. You could, perhaps, set up tours from whichever port they sail into. Include into the tour the usual places in London and then finish with a shoot in the English countryside."

Evelyn felt a tingle of excitement at the base of her spine. "Mr Cameron, thank you. It's an excellent idea! I can see precisely how it would work."

"Lord Clifford would need an injection of capital with no guarantee the scheme would work. I understand that might be difficult in his circumstances."

It would be impossible, but perhaps with help from some of his friends, he could get such a plan off the ground. "Yes, perhaps. I will discuss your suggestions with my husband. For now, I should make my telephone calls."

Stanley Cameron inclined his head slightly and Evelyn

moved past him into the small butler's room. She had never made a telephone call in her life – but Mr Cameron did not need to know that. Her intention was to sit in the room for a few minutes before going back upstairs to speak to Clara Balfour.

CHAPTER 11

Tommy made no pretence of waiting around to speak to Edwin Granville. He simply walked into the drawing room and asked if he could speak to him in the billiard room.

The older man got to his feet and followed Tommy along the corridor. "Do you think they will give us permission to go home soon, Northmoor?"

"Have you spoken to Detective Sergeant Bishop today? I should think he has a better answer for you than I."

Edwin waved a dismissive hand. "He wanted to know where I was from late last night until this morning. Quite a ridiculous question. Obviously, I went to bed after dinner and then came down to breakfast this morning. Where else would I go?"

Tommy held open the door to the billiard room and then followed Edwin Granville inside. "*Someone* went outside."

"So I understand." Edwin sat heavily in an armchair. "Terrible business. But it wasn't me."

"Last time we spoke, you said you prefer people to say things as they are. Is that true?"

"Absolutely. I'm too old to be beating around the bush. If you want to ask me something, just get on with it."

"I have been informed that you have been skimming money out of Albert Lewis's business. Specifically, you note an incorrect amount when making up the accounts. The insinuation is that the difference between the deal and the amount you put in the accounts goes into your pocket."

Edwin choked back a shocked laugh. "Well, that's preposterous."

Tommy cocked an eyebrow. "Is it?"

Slowly, Edwin nodded. "I suppose this has come from that upstart Stanley Cameron? He was getting too big for his boots before Albert's death and I suppose now he is in control of the business for the next year he wants rid of me."

"You haven't actually answered the question."

"Perhaps I sometimes get the figures wrong," Stanley said slyly. "It's possible I may have made a few mistakes. I am only human after all."

"Did Mr Lewis find out you were stealing from him?"

"Now see here!" Edwin blustered. "I have just admitted it is possible I may have made a few accounting errors. That's not stealing."

"It is if the proceeds of your mistakes end up in your pocket," Tommy said firmly. "I don't know the correct terms, but I believe what you've been doing is called embezzlement. I should imagine there would be a prison sentence attached to such a crime."

Edwin's face turned puce and for one awful moment, Tommy thought the older man was about to have a heart attack. "Albert was a particularly stingy employer. I don't intend to say any more on the matter."

"That is probably a very intelligent decision." Tommy eyed the man carefully before he continued. "By the way, you may be interested to know that the silver pen you were missing has been found."

"That's good news. I do so love that pen."

"Unfortunately, it was found in the desk where the box of chocolates that ended up on the front doorstep was kept."

"Oh, this is too much. Really too much." Edwin looked around the room wildly as though he expected someone to come forward and help him. He slumped into his chair when he realised he was by himself. "Someone is trying to frame me. That is perfectly obvious. First my cufflink next to Albert's body and now my pen next to poisoned chocolates."

"We don't know they are poisoned yet."

"The police seem quite convinced they are," Edwin retorted.

"Where were you after your arrival at Rochester Park on Christmas Day? From the moment you arrived until you came downstairs for dinner."

"Well, let me see." Edwin looked up to the ceiling as though the answer was printed there. "After I unpacked, I came downstairs and spoke to Albert for a considerable length of time. Business things, you know. Then I went up to change for dinner."

"And at no point did you go across the lawn to the gardener's shed to take out cyanide and poison Mr Lewis? He didn't, for example, find out that you had been stealing from him and threaten to expose you?"

"That did not happen!" Edwin shouted. "Anyone who says it did is a liar."

Tommy tapped his foot on the floor. "Am I to take the word of a man who has already admitted he is a thief?"

"It's the truth, I tell you! I may have miscalculated a few times, but Albert had so much money he didn't miss a little here and there."

"I imagine he trusted you implicitly too, and it didn't occur to him that his long-serving and supposedly faithful accountant was actually lining his own pockets." He could scarcely believe that Edwin was trying to justify his behaviour. "Who was with Albert when you were talking to him after your arrival?"

Edwin looked confused, as though the question might be a trap. Which, of course, it was. "It was just me and Albert."

"Really?" Tommy asked scathingly. "Because both Peter Balfour and Stanley Cameron claim to have been speaking to Albert after their arrival."

"They were not there," Edwin insisted. "It was just Albert and I."

"Strange how all three of you claim an alibi from a man who is no longer here to verify it," Tommy went on. "How very convenient. Only, of course, it isn't. Because you have all used the same alibi, it makes it even more obvious to both me and the police that none of you have an alibi. Any of you could have gone outside at the time you claim to have been speaking to Albert alone."

"I don't know what they were doing," Edwin said, fury coating his words. "But I know I wasn't plotting to kill Albert. Why would I murder him when—"

"When you were making a pretty penny from him." Tommy finished for him. "Unless it is as I've already stated, and he knew what you were up to."

"I don't have to stay here and listen to your insinuations." Edwin pushed himself to his feet and marched towards the door. "I'm only surprised no one has bumped you or your interfering wife off yet."

Tommy made a move after Edwin, but the other man scurried off.

They really needed to bring this investigation to an end. Not only had Constance and Grace's lives been in danger, but now he and Evelyn were being threatened.

He would chase up the calls he had made earlier that day. It was time to get some answers so they could make sense of the information they had and uncover the murderer.

~

*E*velyn intercepted the luncheon tray meant for Clara Balfour and took it up to the room Clara shared with her husband. She balanced it precariously as she knocked on the door. Drops of tea sloshed from the teapot, causing Evelyn to wonder how on earth the maids carried out this task without making a mess.

Peter opened the door and sighed deeply when he saw Evelyn. "I suppose you have come to harass my wife in the same way your husband has been badgering me?"

"I have brought your wife's tray. A woman in her condition needs to keep her strength up. Especially in such trying and difficult times."

"I suppose you are right," he said grudgingly. "Darling, Lady Northmoor has brought your luncheon."

"How very kind." Clara Balfour was sitting up in bed, her blonde hair loose around her shoulders. Far from looking concerned because there was a murderer in the house, she looked radiant. "I asked for a light lunch. I simply can't manage a big meal these days."

Evelyn put the tray down on the side table near Clara. "I do not want to cause you any distress, Mrs Balfour, but your husband is right. I do wish to ask you some questions."

"If it won't ruin my digestion, then I suppose it'll be alright."

"It's very important we know where everyone was when they arrived at Rochester Park on Christmas Day. From arrival to immediately prior to dinner."

Clara tapped a finger on her chin. "Let me see. Our bags were brought up to our room, and Peter and I then went downstairs. Peter chatted to Mr Lewis in the library and I looked through the bookshelves."

"That's not exactly what your husband said."

"I told your husband I spoke with Mr Lewis which my wife has just verified."

"You said you were alone," Evelyn countered.

"It was rather rude of me not to mention that my wife was in the room with me, too. As Lewis and I were talking business, I quite forgot to mention Clara, but she was certainly in the room with me."

"Then what did you both do?"

They looked at each other in confusion. "Well afterwards we went upstairs and got ready for dinner."

"Were you with Mr Lewis for very long?"

"A half-hour or so," Peter said.

"You arrived around four in the afternoon. If we say it took half an hour for your bags to be taken upstairs and you to settle in, then another half an hour to speak to Mr Lewis. That means it took you approximately three hours to get ready for dinner. Does that sound about right?"

Clara tittered. "It sounds quite absurd when you set it out that way. Perhaps we were longer unpacking, and in the library with Mr Lewis. Certainly it doesn't take us three hours to get ready for dinner! What you must understand, Lady Northmoor, is that when we arrived in this house, we did not expect to account for every minute of our time."

"Of course not," Evelyn said demurely. "One doesn't expect to require an alibi for every minute of one's time. Still, that is the position we are all in."

Clara looked down at the bedspread. "Peter told me what happened this morning with the chocolates and your sisters-in-law. He says it quite baffled the police."

"I think it baffled all of us," Evelyn replied. "Constance saw nothing, yet someone seems so certain she did they want to stop her from talking."

"I understood she saw or heard something immediately prior to dinner?" Clara asked in a sharp voice.

"She thinks she might have." Evelyn held out her hands.

"You know how young girls can be. They are very impressionable."

"She probably shouldn't have said anything unless she was sure," Peter said. "If she had identified someone, but wasn't sure, she could've got someone in a lot of needless trouble."

Evelyn looked between the two of them, trying to see if either of them was lying. She couldn't determine even a flicker of suspicion in either of them. "I suppose that is how we all feel about Lord Clifford. He is at the police station only because this is his house."

"That's not entirely correct, Lady Northmoor." Peter held up a hand. "Lord Clifford has a jolly solid motive."

Evelyn met his gaze steadily. "I don't think there is a person in this house who doesn't have a motive."

"Do you include us in that?" Clara asked.

"I'm afraid I do, Mrs Balfour."

Clara pulled herself a little higher up the bed. "I think I should like my lunch now."

"Certainly." Evelyn walked towards the door. "One more thing. I understand your husband locked you in this room earlier today. Is that correct?"

"For my own safety." Clara looked at Peter adoringly. "Am I not incredibly lucky to have such an attentive husband?"

Attentive wasn't the word Evelyn would have used. Controlling perhaps explained his behaviour better. Tommy was an attentive husband and, if she were afraid, he would stay close by her side to reassure her. He certainly wouldn't have locked her in a bedroom of a strange house and gone about his daily business.

"Do excuse me. I should see about my own meal."

"Thank you for taking the time to bring mine up for me," Clara said sweetly.

They had barely finished lunch when a noise in the corridor announced the return of Detective Inspector Gregory.

Elise flung her napkin on the table and rushed out of the dining room. Her little scream of delight proclaimed better than any words that Hugh had returned home with the detective.

Tommy shook his friend's hand enthusiastically. "I'm so glad you are back."

"As am I, Northmoor." Hugh held Elise close to his side. "It seems you are not the only person happy to see my return."

"Oh, darling." Elise leaned her head against Hugh's shoulder. "I have been positively miserable without you."

"This is all very touching," Detective Inspector Gregory said drily. "However, it doesn't change the fact that our investigations are ongoing. Lord Clifford is still our primary suspect."

"Good afternoon, Sir," Detective Sergeant Bishop walked into the hall. "Do you still want me to travel back to the station with the evidence from this morning?"

"Indeed I do." Gregory nodded emphatically. "Perhaps we should discuss the outcome of your interviews before you leave."

The telephone rang, and it was all Tommy could do to force himself to gaze disinterestedly in its direction. Was this the answer they were waiting for about Clara's first husband?

Malton stepped towards the device but was intercepted by the senior detective. He motioned to his junior colleague, who walked over and lifted the receiver.

"Lord Northmoor?" he said questioningly. "He is here but you may give a message to me, and I shall pass it on."

"I insist I should take my own telephone calls." Tommy

held out his hand for the telephone. Bishop looked at Gregory, who shrugged, then gave a reluctant nod. Neither of them attempted to give him even the illusion of privacy. "Northmoor speaking."

He listened to the caller, taking care not to repeat any of the information they gave him before giving his thanks and replacing the receiver.

"Well?" Gregory asked.

"Well?" Tommy repeated.

"What information have you learned?"

"It was a personal telephone call."

"Lord Northmoor, please do not insult my intelligence. You have a very expressive face. It is clear to me that you have learned information that I insist you share with me."

"Perhaps we should go somewhere private," Evelyn suggested as she exited the dining room to stand next to Tommy.

"Let us go into the library," Gregory suggested.

Tommy and Evelyn followed the two detectives and sat next to each other on the mahogany sofa. It was every bit as uncomfortable as it looked.

"Lord Northmoor?" The detective looked at Tommy as soon as the door was closed. "What have you just found out?"

"The name of Clara Balfour's first husband."

"What is the relevance?"

"I don't know," he allowed. "Not yet anyway."

"Why did you take the time to find out his name?"

"It seemed necessary to me to find out as much as possible about each suspect." Tommy tried to keep his voice as non-committal as possible. *Surely this was standard investigative work.*

"It is for the police force." Gregory looked at him pointedly. "Which you and your wife are not."

"You've been away." Tommy shrugged. "I thought you would appreciate the help."

"I work for the Derbyshire Constabulary, Lord Northmoor. We are extremely capable of investigating without outside interference."

"Forgive me," Tommy said icily. "But you asked me to come in here and tell you what I knew."

"What is he called?" Gregory snapped. "Mrs Balfour's first husband. What is his name?"

"Cecil York."

"Does that name mean anything to you?"

"No." Tommy watched the detective's face – he wasn't the only one who had trouble hiding his emotions from his expression. "Do you recognise the name?"

"I do not." He leaned forward, his eyes on Evelyn. "Lady Northmoor?"

"I recognise the name. I think it's because his surname is York and that is also the name of a town near to where we live."

"That's very helpful, Lady Northmoor," he said patronisingly.

"Don't be rude." Evelyn glared at him. "That's why his name sticks in my mind but it wouldn't unless there was a reason for me to have heard his name before."

"And where did you hear of Cecil York?"

"I wish I could remember."

"Clara Balfour married Cecil York at St Leonards church in Shoreditch, London. Does that help?" Tommy repeated the information he had been given.

"No." Evelyn frowned. "I simply can't recall why I've heard his name before. Perhaps we need to find out more about his death to help in our investigation."

"Whose investigation?" Gregory barked. "I have already warned you about interfering. Do I need to arrest you both for impeding a police enquiry?"

"I should think you will find it difficult to make that charge stick," Tommy said lightly. "We have done nothing to prevent you finding the perpetrator."

In fact, he had deliberately left evidence in two places now – the cufflink next to Albert Lewis's body and the silver pen in the desk next to the boxes of chocolates. He didn't doubt that Elise would have told the police the pen was not hers. It wasn't his fault the detectives were not as fastidious as Elise's housemaids.

Tommy looked at his watch. If they hurried, it might be possible for them to speak to Somerset House and find out more about Cecil York's death. He wasn't sure if it would help, but it was the only lead they had.

"I'm sorry," the detective said, his voice dripping sarcasm. "Are we keeping you?"

"As it happens, yes," Tommy answered. "Come along, darling. I find I would like something sweet after lunch. Let's go down to the kitchen and see if Mrs O'Connell has baked any shortbread."

As they left the library, Evelyn caught hold of his arm. "I take it we are going to use the telephone?"

"We are," Tommy said grimly. "That man's attitude makes me even keener to find the murderer before him."

"Can David help?"

Tommy thought for a moment. "I'm not sure. Let's ask him. He knows so many people in London perhaps he can think of someone to telephone who might help."

Malton stepped forward. "Can I help, My Lord?"

"Yes," Tommy said decisively. "Please ask Mr Ryder to meet me and Lady Northmoor at the telephone in the butler's room."

"Can you feel it?"

"Feel what?" he turned to Evelyn, puzzled by her question.

"The excitement we get when we think we are on to something."

He smiled indulgently. "I'm not sure I care what has brought the colour back into your cheeks. I am just glad to see you looking better. Earlier I thought I might need to call the doctor out to you."

"Stop fussing," she said, but her smile told him Evelyn was grateful for his concern.

CHAPTER 12

The three of them hurried downstairs to the telephone. Evelyn could almost see the moment in the drawing room when they would uncover the murderer. *They were so close!*

"What are we doing?" David asked as they reached the butler's room.

"We need to ask your friend who went to Somerset House for us to go back."

"Today?" David lifted a doubtful eyebrow.

"Certainly today," Tommy said insistently. "I don't want to spend another night in this house with the murderer wondering around poisoning things at will."

"Quite." David rushed through the open door and over to the telephone. "It will be wonderful for Hugh to be cleared of all suspicion. The poor fellow needs to find some way of rebuilding his life."

"You also need to find out about the cyanide, Tommy," Evelyn said. "It's taking Partridge an awful long time to get back to you."

Tommy hit a hand against his forehead. "I am such a fool. I forgot to make the call!"

"It's crucial information, Tommy." Evelyn pulled the door closed behind them. "How could you possibly have forgotten?"

"I was downstairs making the call to arrange for David's friend to visit Somerset House when Alex prevented Constance and Grace from eating the chocolates. After that upset, telephoning Partridge went completely out of my mind."

"Goodness me, Tommy, we shall have to make a list for you in the future."

"I feel about as scatter-brained as Edwin Granville!"

"I don't think you need to exaggerate." Evelyn smiled. "Though let's not forget, that gentleman is clever enough to steal from his employer for years and not get caught."

"He's been stealing?" David enquired.

"We will fill you in later," Tommy promised. "Now let's call your friend and beg for his help."

David made the call but could only speak to his chum's butler. He explained the situation, and the man promised he would either get a message to David's friend or make the journey to Somerset House himself.

"Tell him how urgent it is," Evelyn whispered. "This errand could literally be life or death."

David replaced the receiver and moved out of the way so Tommy could put a telephone call through to Hessleham Hall.

His estate manager, Jack Partridge, lived in a cottage on the grounds. After waiting for anxious minutes, Evelyn could hear Partridge's voice faintly over the line.

"I'm afraid not," Tommy said in response to something Partridge said. "There's been a murder. I need your help."

There was a pause as Partridge answered.

"You may be able to answer my question yourself, or you may need to ask Joe Noble." Tommy rushed on. "It's like this: a chap has been poisoned by cyanide taken from the gardener's shed. We need to know whether it is safe to handle with bare hands or whether one would wear gloves. Is cyanide kept in a packet, or a tin? And, finally, how do you think it would likely be transported from the shed to the house?"

This time, there was a longer pause while Partridge spoke. Evelyn wished there was some way she could hear every word that was spoken by the estate manager instead of having to wait until Tommy finished his conversation. Hearing only one side was incredibly frustrating.

"Yes," Tommy said. "I see. That makes sense. How about something like a vase?"

Again, a silence.

Followed by a brief smile of gratification from Tommy. "You've been extremely helpful, Partridge, thank you. Yes, I shall see you in a couple of days at the most."

"Well?" Evelyn asked impatiently as soon as Tommy replaced the receiver.

"Partridge says no one in their right mind would touch cyanide without wearing gloves. I don't suppose we can find out whether the gardener left gloves in the shed or if the murderer was prepared and took a pair with them."

"I'm certain the missing vase was used," Evelyn said. "It makes sense. What a wonderful cover story if they were seen. They could simply claim they were outside gathering either holly or mistletoe to put into the vase."

"Is the vase opaque?"

"Yes."

"It's evilly genius." Tommy shook his head in wonder. "Even if the person were seen coming back into the house with a vase containing cyanide, they could still claim to be doing some sort of gardening task because it wouldn't be seen."

"We need to find the vase," Evelyn said urgently. "The police could test it for residue, wouldn't they?"

"I believe so." Tommy frowned. "I suppose we are going to have to tell Detective Inspector Gregory this information?"

"We must," Evelyn replied. "I also think we will need their help to set up a little scenario in the drawing room to draw the murderer out."

"I hate it when we have to do that," he said morosely. "They always think they can claim some sort of credit."

Evelyn laughed. "They are always the ones to haul the murderer off in handcuffs so the police always take credit for our hard work."

"Wait." David put a hand on the door. "Does this mean you know who did it?"

"Yes." Evelyn nodded with certainty.

"Can you prove it?"

"That's a completely different question," Tommy said. "But we think we know enough to trick the murderer into a confession."

"You are not going to tell me, are you?" David asked.

"Where is the fun in that?" Tommy asked with a chuckle. "You can find out along with everyone else."

"When will this happen?"

"Oh, before dinner I think."

"Definitely before dinner," Tommy agreed grimly. "No sense in giving the fiend another opportunity to tamper with food."

~

Afternoon tea was set out in the drawing room, and everyone was gathered together. Tommy and Evelyn moved to the front of the room. To the side of the fireplace, Detective Inspector Gregory looked ill at ease.

Tommy was all too well aware that the detective had only agreed to their suggestion because he believed they would fall flat on their faces and look ridiculous in front of their friends and family. He still strongly believed that Hugh was the killer.

"As usual," Tommy began. "This mystery began with a jumble of clues, half-truths, lies, and a dastardly crime. The killer in this case is particularly dangerous and chose an exceptionally cruel way to kill Albert Lewis."

Louisa Lewis drew out her handkerchief and dabbed at the skin underneath her eyes – which Tommy could see even across the room was dry. Still, he could remember the sympathy he had for her when he realised what a difficult life she had led being married to the dead businessman.

"Perhaps we shall start with you, Mrs Lewis?"

"Start with me?" She looked around the room, a shocked expression on her pinched face. "Whatever do you mean?"

"This is a little parlour game Lord and Lady Northmoor have made up," the detective said sardonically. "I will allow them to continue their charade for now. Please play along, Mrs Lewis."

Tommy drew in a deep breath. "There is nothing amusing about a heinous murder, Detective Inspector. This is a very serious matter."

The detective flushed and made a motion with his hand. "Get on with it."

"Until the day after your husband's death, you had no reason to suspect that you were not your husband's beneficiary. Is that correct?"

"I *should* have been left everything after what that man put me through during our marriage," said Louisa bitterly. "But I wouldn't have killed him. Not even for his money."

"You readily accepted that you didn't have an alibi for the afternoon of Christmas Day. You could have easily gone out to the gardener's shed to get the cyanide. No one had a better opportunity than you to poison your husband's tablets."

"That is very true," Louisa said easily. "I can't argue with anything that you've said. It could have been me and at the time of Albert's death, I had a rather excellent motive. The only problem with your hypothesis is that wasn't me. I didn't do it."

Tommy gave a slight nod to acknowledge Louisa's words and turned to Hugh. "I shall deal with you quickly, Lord Clifford. Although the police believe you to be the most likely murderer, I have never subscribed to that idea. You had reason to be furious with Albert Lewis when you found out he had used your need to enter into a lucrative business deal to finagle an invitation to Rochester Park."

"It was a cruel ruse."

"I agree." Tommy glanced quickly at the detective – his face was impassive. "It was egocentric. However, you had no time after finding out he had no intention of buying land from you to go outside and find the cyanide. Therefore, I do not believe you had anything to do with the death of Mr Lewis."

"How convenient given Lord Clifford is your friend that you do not think him capable of murder," Peter Balfour snapped.

"Shall we discuss your motive?" Tommy turned his angry gaze onto the lawyer.

"Yes, let's." Peter met his glare with one of his own. "This should be interesting."

"You're very arrogant for a man who is essentially professionally ruined," Tommy said mildly – his calm voice letting his words carry the greatest weight.

"I am not!" Peter retorted adamantly.

"I'm afraid so," Tommy argued. "You will not get work anywhere else after the events of the last few days."

"You cannot prove a thing." Peter folded his arms across his chest.

Clara put a hand on her husband's thigh. "Peter worked for Mr Lewis for years. I don't understand why you are attacking his character in this way."

"Because, Mrs Balfour, your husband is a fraud. He is not a qualified solicitor."

Peter flicked a piece of lint from his trousers and did his best to look unconcerned. "Like I said, good luck proving your theory."

"You have that the wrong way about." Tommy pinned the man with a stare. "Once word gets about that you do not have the necessary qualifications, you will need to prove that you do to get another job. Can you do that?"

Peter opened his mouth, then closed it again.

"Peter?" Clara questioned. "Darling?"

"I can do the work," he insisted. "I have been doing it for years."

"That's not quite the same thing, is it?"

"I didn't kill Albert," Peter said sulkily.

"Are you telling us that Mr Lewis didn't find out about your lack of qualifications?"

"He didn't," Peter insisted.

"I don't suppose we can ever prove that one way or the other." Tommy lifted a shoulder in defeat. "But it gives you a powerful motive to kill him, doesn't it? And you don't have an alibi. Strangely, both yourself, Edwin Granville, and Stanley Cameron all used Mr Lewis as their pre-dinner alibi. Convenient given the poor man can't disprove it."

"But I was talking to him," Edwin Granville cut in. "I am the only one telling the truth."

"As I said," Tommy said smoothly. "We will never know. After all, we can't ask Albert Lewis for confirmation, can we?"

"You will just have to take my word for it then," Edwin said smugly.

"Shall we talk about your motive next?"

"You can if you like. It proves nothing."

"As I said in our previous conversation, embezzlement is a serious offence."

"Embezzlement?" Detective Inspector Gregory enquired. "Can you prove it?"

"*I* can," Stanley Cameron said. "I have been gathering evidence for months. I intended to present the proof of Granville's guilt to Mr Lewis in the new year."

"Don't listen to anything this guttersnipe says!" Edwin stared furiously at Stanley. "He was nothing until Mr Lewis gave him a job. He has always been jealous of me and the position of trust that I held."

Tommy held up a hand. "We will get to Mr Cameron in time. For now, Mr Granville, shall we concentrate on you?"

"It doesn't matter what I say, does it? This farce will continue unabated, I'm sure."

"You have known Albert Lewis for years and were no doubt aware he took tablets regularly for his blood pressure. You have a motive and no alibi."

"Why would I kill Albert?" Edwin sneered. "With him dead, I had no job. It was never likely these two would keep me on. I've seen them whispering away together. They probably plotted together to kill him. After all, *she* is the one with all of Albert's money."

~

"Let us talk about Miss Mountjoy," Evelyn said. "Or, as we should correctly address her, Mrs Cameron."

A collective gasp sounded around the room. Emma flushed, then gave a negligent shrug. "I don't suppose keeping our marriage secret is necessary anymore, is it?"

Her gaze was on her husband, and it was he who answered her question. "No, darling, it doesn't matter. We know we didn't kill Albert. That's all that matters."

"Neither of you has an alibi for the afternoon before Albert Lewis was killed," Evelyn began. "You both had equal reason to want him dead."

"He was my father!" Emma cried.

"Your what?" Louisa screamed furiously.

"Albert Lewis was my father," Emma repeated quietly. "You insisted he leave London and live in the country to get away from a woman. That woman is my mother."

"That is why your father left you his money," Evelyn said gently. "It appears he felt guilty that he did not feel able to recognise you as his child during his lifetime, but he made sure he provided for you upon his death."

"This is absurd." Louisa sat back heavily in her seat. "How could he have a child I knew nothing about? He didn't want children."

"He wanted *me*," Emma insisted. "He gave my mother money to ensure I had a good education. If he didn't want me, he would not have left me his money."

"Of course, this means you had a stronger motive than anyone," Evelyn said calmly. "Your father's death leaves you an extremely wealthy woman."

"It does," Emma agreed. "But I would rather have had a father. He was teaching me so much."

"I can't believe this." Louisa pulled out her handkerchief and this time her tears were real. "All these years he hid this from me."

"I am sorry, Mrs Lewis, desperately sorry for your pain." Emma looked at her father's wife with compassion, but the widow refused to look her way.

"You have no alibi for—"

"She was with me," Stanley cut in. "We were together. Obviously, no one will believe us but that is the truth."

"And your motive, Mr Cameron, is as strong as your wife's. Albert Lewis's death leaves your wife and, by extension, you an exceedingly rich man."

"It does," Stanley agreed. "But as Emma said, that's no substitute for having Mr Lewis alive. He gave me a chance to make something of myself. I owe him everything. Goodness only knows what would have become of me if he hadn't taken me under his wing. I would *never* repay him by taking his life."

"You've been quiet, Mrs Balfour," Evelyn commented.

"I'm simply taking it all in," Clara said calmly. "It's quite remarkable that everyone seems to have a little secret they would rather stay hidden."

"Including yourself?"

"I have no secrets," she said firmly.

"Not even your first husband?"

Clara tossed her head and smiled prettily. "My husband died in extremely sad circumstances. That has no relevance to Mr Lewis's death."

"On the contrary," Evelyn said. "What was his name?"

"His…his name?" Clara faltered. "Why does that matter?"

"What was his name, Mrs Balfour?"

"I—"

"We know his name." Evelyn took in Clara's shocked expression. "Yes, we could confirm with Somerset House that you married your husband at St Leonard's Church in Shoreditch and his name was Cecil York."

Clara closed her eyes in despair. The room fell silent as everyone tried to work out the significance of the dead man's name.

"I know that name!" It was Alex Ryder who spoke. "His death was quite the scandal."

"It was not," Clara insisted. "He died of gastroenteritis. That is what his death certificate says."

Evelyn took a calming breath. This was the most important part of their presentation. She *needed* Clara Balfour to believe what she said so they could catch her out.

"We are waiting for a telephone call from the doctor who signed poor Cecil's death certificate. He didn't believe his death was from natural causes, did he?"

"He did his best to blacken my name at the inquest, but he was unsuccessful."

Alex snapped his fingers. "That's why I remember the case. Your picture was in the newspaper. My chums and I made a rather crass joke that if we were going to be poisoned by a wife, we could only hope that it was one as attractive as you."

Clara smiled despite the seriousness of the discussion. "How sweet."

Alex shot an apologetic look at Constance, but she missed the glance, as her attention was taken completely by Clara Balfour.

"The doctor is seeking permission from the court to have Cecil's body exhumed and the necessary tests performed."

"They won't be able to prove a thing."

Evelyn didn't know if it was even possible for tests to be carried out after all this time, but she needed her bluff to shake Clara enough for the woman to make a mistake. She crossed her fingers behind her back.

"Perhaps not. However, your fingerprints on the green vase missing from this room will be proof that you were the person who went out to the gardener's shed and used it to transport cyanide into the house."

"Lady Northmoor! What a fanciful imagination you have."

"Your *fingerprints* and the residue of cyanide inside the vase will be enough to convict you of the death of Albert Lewis."

"You don't have the vase."

"Oh, you hid it well." Evelyn smiled. "Just not well enough."

"I don't believe you."

"I'm sure you don't *want* to believe it." She turned to Constance. "Do you still have your chocolates?"

Constance reached under her seat and drew out a box of chocolates. "Yes, here it is."

She carried it over to Evelyn and handed it over. Evelyn opened the box and walked forward and offered the sweets to Clara. "Choose one, Mrs Balfour."

"No."

"Why not?"

"I thought the police took the chocolates away because they were contaminated."

"They thought we were paranoid, so didn't remove them from the house as planned." Evelyn lifted a shoulder. "Are we paranoid, Mrs Balfour, or is there a reason you won't take a chocolate from the box you left on the doorstep for Constance?"

"I did not," she denied, but the fight and certainty had gone from her voice. "It wasn't me."

"Who was it then? Your husband? Did he kill Mr Lewis to keep your secret safe?"

"Cyril died of stomach flu," Peter said weakly. "You told me that, darling. That *is* the truth, isn't it?"

"Of course it is," Clara snapped.

"Did you kill Albert Lewis?" Evelyn looked at Peter. "Then did you sneak out while your wife was sleeping to leave a poisoned box of chocolates for Constance, believing she had seen you the night before when you were out getting the cyanide?"

Peter looked at his wife with tears in his eyes. "It can't have been me. I struggle to sleep in strange houses, so I took a sleeping draught. It wasn't me. Why won't you take a chocolate, Clara? You love sweets."

"For goodness' sake, Peter!" Clara exploded. "You're so pathetically weak."

"No." Peter put his hands over his ears and shook his head. "No! I don't want to hear any more."

Clara slapped his hands away. "Well, you're going to hear

all of it. That disgusting man approached me when we arrived and told me he remembered seeing the case in the newspaper. He was going to tell you and ruin everything."

"I'm your husband," Peter said desperately. "I would have believed whatever you told me. I believed you when you told me about Cyril. We're having a baby! Oh, Clara, why did you do it?"

"You stupid man," she spat. "I did it for me. I didn't want the past being dragged back up and risk someone insisting on reopening Cyril's death like these people have done."

Evelyn looked around at Detective Inspector Gregory, who stood stupefied, his mouth half open like a fish on the end of a line. "Detective?"

He moved like a sleepwalker over to the door and opened it. "Constable, get in here."

A uniformed officer walked into the room and looked enquiringly at the detective.

"No!" Clara screamed. "You can't prove a thing!"

"Arrest that woman," the detective instructed, "for the murder of Albert Lewis and the attempted murder of Miss Constance Christie."

The police officer led Clara from the room in handcuffs. They could hear her screaming her innocence until the heavy front door shut behind her.

"I say," Aunt Em said. "I assume those are not the poisoned chocolates. If I am correct, I would rather like a sweet and a large gin and tonic."

"The tainted box has indeed gone off to the station in Derby, Lady Emily," the detective said. "Those are quite safe to eat."

"Then let us all have one and a good stiff drink," she said. "After that performance I have absolutely no desire for tea and dainty sandwiches."

EPILOGUE

"But how did you know?" Constance pressed Evelyn later that afternoon when the family, together with Stanley and Emma Cameron, were sitting in the drawing room.

"It made sense that she was the one," Evelyn said. "She not only had most to lose, but the crime was desperate. It was something Emma said that made me rethink everything we thought we knew."

"What was it?" Emma asked.

"You said that if you wanted to kill Albert, you could have done it at any time after finding out he was leaving his estate to you. That made me think about who had an immediate need for him to die."

"Yes. If Stanley or I wanted Albert dead, we had countless opportunities to create an accident as we worked together every single day."

"I spoke to Mr Balfour about the manner of death," Tommy said. "I suggested that poison was premeditated and not a sudden loss of control. Of course, that is true. But we realised that *something* must have happened to make the killer so frantic they took exceptional risks to kill him."

"Nothing had changed, you see," Evelyn went on. "For every other suspect, nothing was any different on Christmas Day than it had been on any other day leading up to the visit to Rochester Park."

"But Albert Lewis recognised Clara Balfour." Tommy paused to take a breath. "We think he realised as soon as he saw her on Christmas Day. It frightened her into taking drastic action."

"But how did you know about her husband?" Aunt Em asked.

"We didn't," Evelyn admitted with a little laugh. "We knew his name and where they were married. The part about his body being exhumed was an elaborate bluff. We hoped Clara wouldn't be able to cope with the presume and, of course, she couldn't."

"Neither has the vase been found," Tommy confessed. "Even if the police locate it, we think Clara would have worn gloves. I spoke to Partridge earlier, and he was very certain that no one would handle cyanide without wearing gloves. I neglected to ask the question, but I would assume there would be some sort of warning on the packaging to that effect."

"You were taking an enormous risk, Northmoor," Alex said with disapproval.

"We were certain our theory was correct," Evelyn said quietly. "All we had to do was make Clara think we knew more than we did and could prove at least some of what we were saying."

"What do you think will happen to her?" Emma asked.

"Her attractiveness and the fact she is having a baby shouldn't matter, but I'm afraid that both will count in her favour." Tommy twisted his face in consternation. "A jury will not want to send a woman like Clara Balfour to her death."

"And yet they must," Emma insisted. "She killed my father."

"I think the Crown Prosecution Service will put forward an alternate charge to murder," David suggested. "Something that Clara will admit to with no trial. A crime that does not carry the death penalty."

Emma shook her head. "Whatever happens to her, I still think she will get away lightly after what she did to my father."

"I think we are in agreement, my dear." Aunt Em looked around the room with a mischievous gleam in her eye. "Now, who is for another drink?"

Alex moved into the centre of the room in front of the fireplace. "I have something I would like to say."

Evelyn slipped her hand into Tommy's, and they exchanged a smile. They both knew exactly what Alex Ryder was about to say.

"Constance," he began, then cleared his throat. "Miss Constance Christie. Since the moment I saw you, I have been unable to stop thinking about you. Goodness only knows how hard I have tried. I never expected to be one of those men who were silly romantic fools over a woman. One who was ruled by his emotions without a sensible thought in his head. But now I am proud to say that I adore you beyond comprehension. I cannot imagine allowing a single day passing by without having you in my life."

"Oh," Grace breathed. "How romantic."

Alex moved forward and dropped on to one knee before Constance. He extracted a velvet box from the inside pocket of his jacket. "I know we haven't known each other for very long and I understand you may need some time to think about your answer, but I am prepared to wait. Forever, actually, for your answer. So long as the answer is yes."

"Lord Chesden," Constance whispered. "You haven't asked me anything yet."

He flushed, then opened the box. "I don't deserve such a

wonderful, sweet, and beautiful woman like you to look at me twice but—"

"Alex." Constance reached out a hand to cup his face. "Please just ask the question."

"Constance, will you do me the very great honour of becoming my wife?"

"I shall need some time to think about my answer."

"Yes, of course." He snapped the box closed, unable to prevent a look of defeat from taking over his face.

"I've thought about it," Constance said. "It's yes! A thousand times, yes!"

"Malton!" Aunt Em called. "Put away the gin. Lord Clifford, I do hope there is champagne in this house, and lots of it!"